Huddle Up

Little Hondo Press
Contact: littlehondopress@yahoo.com

Huddle Up

Also by Liz Matis

Playing For Keeps – print, eBook, and audio book

Love By Design – print, eBook, and audio book

Going For It – print, eBook and audio book

Real Men Don't Drink Appletinis – eBook

Praise for Liz Matis

Love By Design

RT Book Review: Readers will get a kick out of these characters as they walk through a world of fashion and celebrities and soak up all the glitz and glam that a wild child and a bad boy could possibly provide.

Love on the Book Shelf: Don't hold this book too tight-you-you'll burn your fingers. **Recommendation:** It's also the perfect just-before-bedtime reading, if you'd like some nice, sultry dreams.

ReRead: Totally worth it.

Playing For Keeps – Fantasy Football – Season 1

RT Book Reviews: Playing For Keeps is entertaining ... an engaging storyline will keep readers turning the pages ... readers will enjoy the unfolding relationship and anticipate the sequel featuring the secondary characters

Book Junkie: In Liz Matis' latest from Little Hondo Press, Playing For Keeps you will get a wildly sexy romance with depth and laughs. A page turner, bring on the sequel.

Going For It – Fantasy Football – Season 2

RT Book Reviews: Readers will wholeheartedly enjoy the cat-and-mouse game the main couple plays. Expect a large dose of spice, surprises, and a story that's perfect for the front page of a tabloid. The sequel to Playing For Keeps is a touchdown!

Book Junkie: I loved GOING FOR IT because falling hard and fast for two witty, feisty and completely honest characters that do nothing if not capture your heart and take you on the wild ride that is their love story.

Huddle Up

Fantasy Football – Season 3

By Liz Matis

To Angel, Love Billy – August 2007

Angels arrive on a
ray of light
they say
My Angel arrived on a
moonbeam
one hot summer night
and remained
earthbound
once upon my mortal kiss

Chapter 1

Less than twenty-four hours ago Billy Burner discovered he'd fathered a child. Maybe. Now he stood outside O'Malley's Pub clutching the demand for a court-ordered DNA test in his hand.

His playbook didn't have a section on fatherhood. The chapter on greedy, conniving women he knew by heart. So why hadn't Angel sued him for child support after he signed his first pro contract two years ago? And why had she waited until now, six years after he'd last seen her, to spring a kid on him? It must be a lie. Only the date of birth nagged at his conscious. Had their teenage summer romance produced a love child? He wanted answers and wanted them in person. Face to face.

Or did you just need the excuse to see her again? No way.

His agent, Carlos, had advised him not to come to the small Ohio town where he once attended football camp, warning him it was a ploy for his money or at the very least for attention. Carlos was probably right. God, Billy hoped so. With the final preseason game only days away, he needed the matter settled so he could have a clear head. The head coach of the NY Cougars gave him forty-eight hours to be back on the field. And that was twelve hours ago.

Opening the door, he shut his watering eyes against the reek of stale tobacco, spilled beer, and another scent he couldn't quite place. God, it smelled worse than the locker room. With his manicured fingers, he pinched the bridge of his nose to ward off the stench. He stepped into the bar area, his Italian shoes crunching peanut shells with every footfall. The custom-made suit fit him like armor, strong enough to block any female tactics Angel might employ.

The bartender, who was big and bad enough to step in and play on any defensive line, hadn't changed a bit. Hoss even wore the same battered leather biker vest. "Well look who has the balls to show up here."

"Huge ones." In enemy territory Billy knew when to go on the offensive. "Where's Angel?"

Hoss hurdled over the bar and planted himself in front of him. The attempt at intimidation almost made him roll his eyes. As a tight end Billy faced off every Sunday against a line of men who wanted to break his legs.

"If you hurt her, you'll be answering to me," Hoss warned.

Hurt Angel? Billy held in a laugh at the absurdity of it. It was he who needed protection from her cutting words that had stabbed his once tender teenage heart. Now women claimed he didn't have one.

Billy weaved his way through the Tuesday night crowd to the back room where four regulation-sized pool tables sat. Various framed billiard posters graced the walls. His favorite, a group of dogs shooting pool still hung in the same spot above the jukebox. Cigarette smoke swirled in the air, hazing the bright lights hanging above the tables.

The 'no smoking' laws didn't apply to an illegal pool hall like O'Malley's.

Her laughter filled the air. Memories of those hot summer nights in her arms reeled through his mind like a highlight film. Drawn to the sound, his gaze searched for the girl he once loved. Glued to the spot in the doorway, he was fairly certain it wasn't from the gum stuck on the sole of his shoe.

Angel O'Malley leaned across the pool table, her breasts nearly grazing the green felt. Her blouse gaped, exposing the porcelain sheen of her skin. It was perhaps the only angelic thing about her. Then again wasn't porcelain glazed at very high temperatures? Her raven hair tumbled over one shoulder, a black as sin waterfall cascading into the river Styx.

He suspected he wasn't the only man more interested in how she filled out those tight jeans than in the game in progress. With her bewitching green eyes fixed upon the nine ball and her slender fingers cradling the cue stick, she stretched across the table and lined up a nearly impossible shot. He held his breath in anticipation as she slowly drew back the stick. She hit the cue ball with a driving force that sent the nine ball on its planned trajectory. It spun for the side pocket like a perfect spiral hurled by a quarterback. When the ball sank, high-fives and money were exchanged.

"Who's next?" she shouted. She lifted a beer to the first lips he'd ever kissed.

"I am," he bellowed.

The buzz of the bar fell silent, until only Kid Rock's All Summer Long blared from the jukebox.

He gained a small satisfaction from seeing the bottle halt midway to her mouth. A moment later she faced him with a smile that could seduce the devil. Or him. No, he told himself, that was a teenage boy's memories trying to worm their way back to the surface. He buried the foolish feelings. Billy wasn't that naïve kid anymore.

"What's your game, stranger?" she asked.

The muscle in his jaw twitched. And Hoss thought Billy had balls? Angel not only played games, she stacked the rules in her favor. Six years of silence and now out of the blue a paternity suit. She hadn't bothered to answer the two letters he mailed. He figured she taken off to Vegas the first chance she got and joined the women's pro pool circuit. It was her dream. And he held her back or so she said when she cut him loose. His ego still stung from her parting words, *'Oh, and I faked it.'*

There she stood, still playing pool in her father's dive of a bar and drinking beer. For a moment it felt like he'd stepped back in time. Nothing had changed, except she had a child. His child. Maybe, he reminded himself.

"I don't play games." He strode forward and tossed the court papers onto the pool table. "Why is the mother of my child hustling pool?"

A fleeting moment of hurt etched her beautiful face and Billy regretted his words but then her brows furrowed.

"Everyone out," ordered Angel.

Maybe she didn't want any witnesses, which was fine with him. The paparazzi would crawl up his ass and take pictures of the event if they knew. After the fiasco with fashion's new it girl, his coach had read him the riot act. Billy's job was to play football and his ugly mug belonged on the sports pages not in celebrity rag magazines. But if Angel's angle wasn't to attract media attention, then she wanted money. Why now?

And why after all these years did his heart still race at the mere sight of her. Carlos had been right, Billy should've stayed away and let the lawyers handle it. God, and he'd been worried about female hysterics when he should've been worried about his own state of mind.

Chapter 2

As the crowd filed out of the back room, Angel took a long pull on the first beer she'd had in months. Wasn't it just like the universe's twisted sense of humor to have Billy Burner return on the same night she allows herself to have some adult fun? There he stood, indignant in his misconception, accusing her of hustling pool and child abandonment. *Well, you were hustling. But Billy would know all about child abandonment.* She wouldn't even be hustling if she hadn't needed the money to buy groceries.

Grabbing a cue stick, she chalked the tip with practiced seductive strokes designed specifically to throw off the men she played against. Using her long bangs as a shield, she covertly examined Billy and compared the man in front of her to the memory of the teenage boy she once loved. Six years roughened the boy band cuteness that high school girls once wrote about in their diaries. He'd grown an inch or two, which now meant he had a clear foot over her 5'5" self. She couldn't see the muscles, but thanks to his near naked TV ads for a men's cologne, she knew exactly what lay beneath the suit that would've hung off his seventeen-year-old frame.

His face was devoid of the easy smile with dimples deep enough to get lost in. Instead he wore a determined frown. Only the shaggy blond hair that had come to be his trademark remained. And, of course, the eyes, such a striking cobalt blue that she'd only known one other human to possess. Her daughter. With that thought her weakening knees straightened and so did her backbone.

"You too, Hoss. Out." The bartender was more of a family friend than an employee, but this was between her and Billy.

"I'm not leaving you alone with him," he said as he folded his arms.

"Damn Hoss, you really think I could hurt Angel?"

The unmistakable catch in Billy's voice surprised her. Perhaps some part of him still cared. She mentally shook off that silly schoolgirl fantasy. Look where it got her the last time, a candidate for MTV's 16 and pregnant.

"Who knows, deadbeat? Too many hits to your head? Steroids? You wouldn't be the first football player to shoot his girlfriend," Hoss challenged.

"Fine." Billy flashed opened his suit jacket to prove he wasn't carrying, but that didn't seem to satisfy Hoss who frisked him like he made his living as a cop and not a bartender. Billy glared at Angel and she glared right back even though she'd give anything to see that smile again.

What did he have to be mad about? So boo-hoo she'd sued him for child support. She wouldn't have asked for even a penny if she weren't about to be evicted. When the news aired videos showing Billy raining money on strippers and on his supermodel girlfriend who had joined them up on stage, Angel had enough of scraping by. The paternity suit she filed days later had nothing to do with jealously, she convinced herself, and was done in the name of fairness. Damn it, she was only doing what was right, only doing what Billy should've been man enough to do.

Hoss straightened and without taking his eyes off of Billy said, "I'll be right outside."

The door shut. Billy held her gaze until the song on the jukebox ended. Silence filled the space where Gabriela was conceived. Not the most auspicious of beginnings for her little girl, but Angel swore she'd provide a better life for the both of them.

"Is it true?" He nodded to the rolled up papers on the pool table.

Stunned, she blinked before narrowing her eyes. "Excuse me?"

"Is it true?"

"What? True that I've been raising our daughter alone? That five years ago you denied you were the father?" Her grip on the cue stick tightened until she thought it would pulverize into sawdust.

"I can't deny something I never knew about."

"Never knew about?" Angel flung the stick to the side and got up in his face. The smell of the cologne he hawked surrounded her like an ocean breeze. The stink of the bar intruded making it easy to ignore the pangs of want. The money he made and wasted from that endorsement deal alone could have paid off Angel's student loans. "Are you claiming my father didn't travel eight hours to tell you I had a baby? That you didn't laugh in his face and call me a whore?"

"No!" Billy gripped her arms. "I would never do that."

His fingers pressed into her flesh. Being this close to him made her weak when she needed to be strong. She yanked away. "Don't touch me."

"I didn't know anything until the court papers showed up. I swear it. Go ask him. Where is O'Malley, anyway? Surprised he's not down here beating me over the head with a pool stick."

Her heart clenched at the sincerity in his voice. It couldn't be true. But what if Billy was telling the truth? What if everything her father had said was a lie? It certainly wouldn't be the first time. But it was one thing to lie about where the bar's profits had disappeared to and quite another to lie about Billy. Where did he go that weekend if not to Billy's hometown? The answer was so simple, so obvious. The casino. Angel turned away from Billy so he couldn't see the tears welling up in her eyes. How could her father do this to her? To Gabby?

She didn't know which truth was worse, Billy denying paternity or that her father lied about it. Wasn't it enough that she broke it off with Billy when O'Malley said if she really loved Billy she'd let him go. And why did a flicker of the burning love they once shared start to flame. Tired of being the strong one, the tears she'd been unable to shed at the funeral spilled down her cheeks. Sobs began to rack her body and Billy wrapped her up in a hug.

"Angel," he whispered into her hair. "What's going on?"

She turned in his arms burying her face in his chest, surely ruining his jacket with her salty tears. Without looking up she said, "He's dead."

Chapter 3

Billy struggled to process the warring emotions raging inside him. Anger. Bitterness. Confusion. Tenderness. The feeling of Angel in his arms won out against all the other long held beliefs. He stroked her hair as he mumbled comforting words. Barging into O'Malleys searching for answers had led to more questions. But only one needed answering at the moment. "Where is Gabriela?"

His daughter's name felt foreign on his lips. According to the paternity suit Angel chose not to use his last name. Why would she when she believed he'd denied parentage? Was he a heartless bastard to be glad O'Malley was dead? He didn't think so, otherwise he never would've learned of Gabriela. Or had the chance to embrace Angel again. For a precious moment time held no meaning.

After one last sniffle, Angel backed away and said, "She's at a princess sleepover."

He could only guess at what that entailed. Though he itched to meet his daughter, perhaps it was for the best that it wouldn't be right away. He and Angel needed to figure out the next step.

"Can we talk somewhere more private?" He nodded towards the door where he knew Hoss waited for a chance to kick his ass. If O'Malley had told him the same lie then Billy couldn't blame him.

"Upstairs." She pointed to the exit leading to the apartments before letting the crowd back in from the main bar area.

Smoking hot memories of sneaking up to her bedroom nearly made him forget the court papers on the pool table. A flurry of whispers from those funneling back inside drowned out Angel's voice, but he heard Hoss' deep baritone call. "Don't do anything stupid."

"I'm not a hormonal teenager anymore," she shouted back before shutting and bolting the back door that connected to the hallway of the residential part of the building.

Angel might not be hormonal, but with his gaze transfixed on her shapely ass as she climbed the stairs, his testosterone shot up to caveman levels. It wasn't the first time he replayed the last night they made love. That night he had shed the fumbling boy who took her virginity, along with his own, in the backseat of his car. Instead he had made love to her long and slow until they both broke out in a glistening sweat.

Entering the apartment, he took note of the same yellow couch standing in the same spot and he half-expected to see O'Malley snoring away in the shabby recliner. Hard to believe the old man was dead. If it weren't for the toys strewn about and a new wall full of photos he would have thought Angel lived in a time capsule of her youth.

Angel broke the silence, "I'll get you a beer."

He could use something stronger, but he nodded. When she left the room, he walked over to the wall displaying his daughter's life. His hand drew up to touch the newborn photo before moving on to a picture of Angel looking young and scared, and holding Gabriela in the hospital. Anger at O'Malley surged up inside him. Billy should have been there.

Witnessing each milestone in 2D nearly brought him to tears. With each photo his daughter grew more beautiful and Angel more confident, both of them happy without him. Though Gabriela wore her hair in long curls, the ebony color matched her mother's. Billy didn't need a DNA test to tell him he was the sperm donor to the unique colored eyes staring back at him. There was no maybe about it; Billy was Gabriela's father.

Would the photos have included him if he knew of Angel's pregnancy? For the first time Billy asked himself what he would've said to O'Malley. As the jilted seventeen-year-old boy would he have accepted his responsibilities? Or would he have said exactly what O'Malley conjured up. Why didn't Angel come to him herself or answer his letters? Unless she never got them. O'Malley must have intercepted them. But why? Her father seemed to like him, unlike Billy's father who had done everything in his power to keep Angel and Billy apart.

Noticing an unframed picture on the end table face down, he picked it up and turned it over. The image of a beaming woman wearing a nurse's uniform and holding a diploma confused him for a moment. Then he realized it was Angel with her glorious dark hair tucked under the cap. Returning to the living room she handed him a beer. Looking grim, she took the photo out of his hand and placed it back on the table, again face down. Why? She should be proud.

"You're a nurse?" Billy took a swig of the beer. Yeah, he really needed something stronger.

Angel shrugged. "Yes, and no. I still have to take the licensing exam."

Billy couldn't help but be impressed. While he'd concentrated on making a name for himself in college football and then the NFL, Angel, with her dreams of being a professional pool player shattered, had raised a daughter, earned a degree, and no doubt did so while helping her father in the dive downstairs. In comparison his Liberal Arts education seemed uninspiring. His academics took a backseat to the game of football. He studied game films, dissected the opponent's defense, and memorized the playbook. Too bad there wasn't a gridiron degree. He hadn't even finished college and in his junior year had declared himself early for the NFL draft. "When do you take it?"

"I haven't rescheduled yet. O'Malley died the day before the exam." She stepped around the recliner and peered out the window. "I have no money. It's the only reason I filed for child support. O'Malley died two months ago owing everyone."

"Gambling?" It wasn't a question really, not even a guess.

She nodded. "This all belongs to—" Looking away from the window she swept her hand around in a mock gesture, but then dropped her hand to her side. "Well, it's not important."

Three generations of O'Malley's had owned the bar. Angel would've have been the fourth in spite of arguing she'd rather die first. Billy's father wasn't the only one who thought she'd end up on a stripper's pole whether she stayed or took off to Vegas. She may have remained in this downtrodden town, had a baby out of wedlock during her senior year of high school but she didn't end up a statistic and she proved them all wrong by earning a college degree. That took fucking guts.

Time had only toughened the goth girl from the proverbial wrong side of town. She deserved so much more. So did his Gabriela. He looked to the wall of photos. The first few years of his daughter's life had been a financial struggle, but Billy had the power to change all that. It was time for him to set things right.

Taking a deep breath, he readied himself for the big step he was about to take. Releasing the air out of his lungs, he turned back to Angel. The light from the street lamp filtered through the lace curtains creating a soft glow across her face. When does one fall out of love with one's first heartbreak? Never.

So *are you doing this for them or for yourself?* A little of both, but a small part of him hoped he was doing it for the family they could be together. Another larger part thought he was an idiot. Drawn to her like a movie vampire to its female prey, Billy came to stand beside Angel without realizing he'd moved. Taking her hands in his he asked, "Move in with me."

Chapter 4

"Hell no!" The hands that held hers felt like shackles instead of flesh. Angel jerked away and strode to the door, hoping he'd take the hint and leave.

She'd never depend on another man. Her father had either gambled away the profits or drank them. He lied to her over and over again. Billy was probably no different. She might need his child support. Herself, she could take care of just fine.

"I have a right to see my daughter." Billy didn't budge an inch.

Frankly, she didn't care what his rights were but Gabby did deserve to meet her father and have him in her life that she did know. While never worthy of a corny Father of the Year plastic trophy at least O'Malley had stuck around, unlike her mother. That meant something. The void her mother left behind could never be filled. She didn't want that for Gabby. Still, she wasn't going to make it easy for Billy. "Sure, you can see her every other weekend."

"You know that's not going to work. I practice all week and play on Sundays."

"You see? Already putting football above your daughter." She couldn't help the snarky tone lacing her voice.

"That's not fair." His fingers raked through his golden locks in frustration.

Angel remembered applying a lighter touch to his silky hair. Remembered how much she once loved him and how her father manipulated that love to convince her to set him free. Not that she'd ever tell Billy. "Believe me, I'm well versed in what's not fair."

"I know you are, Angel. Raising a kid on your own. Struggling financially." He moved away from the window to pull her from the door and onto the battered couch. "Give yourself a break from all this. Help me to get to know Gabriela."

The sound of her daughter's name coming out of his mouth put fear into her heart. Would he try to take Gabriela away? He had the money to hire a team of lawyers. What did she have but a bar about to be foreclosed on by the mob? "Won't we cramp your style?"

"My style?"

"Strippers, for one." At least there was some ammunition she could use against him if he tried to sue for full custody.

"Keeping tabs on me?"

She didn't like the teasing tone or the thoughtful look that followed it. "Hardly. You're a media whore."

"Ouch."

"The truth hurts." She mentally shrugged off her own irrational hurt feelings of seeing Billy surrounded by strippers.

"I'll give you that one but I can assure you I don't frequent strip clubs." Reaching over he rested his hand on her knee. "Or bring them home."

Their gazes met. Angel nearly choked on the emotion clawing inside her. And God help her, desire too. Did he ever think about their time together? And if he did was it just the sex he remembered? Damn, is that what he wanted right now? By the look in his eyes the answer was yes and she slapped his hand away. "Your supermodel girlfriend won't be pleased."

He laughed. "I don't have girlfriends. You expertly cured me of wanting one."

"Oh." Angel didn't know what to think about that. She scrambled for another reason to put him off this crazy idea.

"What about you? Is there a boyfriend?"

"No," she said without thinking. Damn, that could've been a way to decline his offer. The smug look on his face pissed her off and she recovered with, "Nothing of a permanent nature." Her remark hit its target and he dropped his gaze.

"Then there's no reason for you to stay here." He adjusted the cufflinks on his shirt. "I have three bedrooms if that's what you're worried about."

She wasn't concerned on that front. He'd have to wear a condom over his whole body before she'd let him make love to her. She wouldn't take the chance of getting pregnant again no matter how much her hormones raged. The only fool proof birth control was abstinence, a state of being of which she was an expert. She wouldn't be a woman with babies from multiple men. No way.

"Once Gabriela is comfortable with me, you two can get your own place nearby."

"I can't afford an apartment in New York City and what about the licensing requirements, they differ state to state." Even then, her nurse's salary could never compete with his money. Billy could give Gabby anything and everything.

Again she worried if he would eventually try to get custody. Panic settled in her tightening muscles. She wasn't sure if she should run or fight. Hell, even joint custody would crush her. She reminded herself this wasn't about what she wanted, it's what was best for Gabby and it always would be.

"I live across the river in New Jersey and I'll pay for the apartment."

"I don't need a man—"

"Damn it Angel!" Billy stood and turned to face her. "You sued me for child support."

True, but she wanted a check in the mail every month not the man. The foundation of lies her father built crumbled in an instant and she needed to decide based on her new reality. Still, she needed time to adjust. And space. "New Jersey is a long way from here."

"Years ago you couldn't wait to leave," he said softly, almost in a whisper.

"Yes, I did." She hated this town, hated the people in it who thought she was nothing but trouble and thought she and Billy didn't belong together, including her own father. Right after graduation she was going to take off for Vegas and support herself hustling pool until she made the pro circuit. She allowed herself one more night with Billy and then broke his heart and in the process her spirit. Then she found out she was pregnant and though she was scared she held onto a secret hope that Billy would be happy. Stupid teenager.

Just because O'Malley lied didn't mean Billy would've run to her rescue. He could act like a knight in shining armor now that he was rich and famous. Where was he when it counted? A fleeting moment of bitterness crept in. But she wouldn't trade Gabby for all the money in his bank account. Gabby was her world.

"It might be too much. Her grandfather just died and believe it or not O'Malley doted on her."

"Probably out of guilt."

Angel's earliest memory of her father was of him instructing her to call him O'Malley. As Papa, he offered Gabby piggyback rides and sweets. If he'd been this attentive when Angel was little, she didn't remember it. Calling him Papa in front of Gabby gave Angel some solace to her damaged inner child.

"All I'm asking for is a chance to make things right."

"Out of guilt?" She threw back his words regarding her father against him. She had to know.

Billy knelt at her feet and took her hands in his. "The only thing we were both guilty of is being young."

This time his touch soothed instead of banding like iron. The sincerity of his plea jump-started the inner workings of her heart creating an opening she thought she'd closed forever. Falling in love with him again would be so easy, but she needed to take her emotions out of the equation for her daughter's sake. "Let's see how Gabby reacts. If she is scared or the least bit apprehensive, you'll just have to wait until football season is over."

He nodded in understanding. "Gabby is her nickname?"

"Yeah, she's a talker."

He got off his knees and sat back down on the couch. "Tell me more."

Billy seemed so interested that she was taken aback for a moment, but then she settled in and started telling stories about their daughter. He sat in silence, staring at the wall of photos. She supposed she'd gone a little crazy with the picture taking, but she wanted Gabby to know she was loved. Angel had exactly two pictures from her childhood.

The long day—hell, her life for the past six years—took its toll and she yawned. She snuggled into the blanket encasing her and a kiss feathered across her forehead. Almost like her and Gabby's nighttime ritual in reverse. A sigh escaped her lips. She must be dreaming. No one had ever tucked her in.

The door slammed the next morning and she heard tiny footsteps approaching the couch. Angel played possum then sprung up and pulled her daughter into a tickle-filled hug. The sound of her little girl's laughter made all the struggles and sacrifices worth it.

"Mommy, you're silly. Why are you sleeping on the couch?"

"Did you have a good time?" She may have only been next door but Angel missed her baby.

"Yes!" A plastic pink tiara studded in clear rhinestones slid to the side of her head. "But I missed you. Where's Lucy?"

Angel smiled at the image her daughter made in her pajamas but righted the tiara to proper princess protocol.

"She's in your room." Angel watched as her little princess skipped off, wondering when Billy left and when he'd return. Maybe he came to his senses and ran off. Better now than later. As long as he sent a check, she didn't care. *Liar.*

Angel curled up on the couch with the intention of catching five more minutes of sleep. Then Gabby's scream filled the air. It was either Billy or a spider. As Angel sprung up she hoped for the latter.

Chapter 5

In the hallway Billy stood frozen in front of the pint-sized tiara-wearing banshee. Frozen in shock or terror he couldn't say. Probably both. Seeing her smiling pictures was one thing but being confronted by the live screaming version was another. Should he pick her up? He moved to do so and the pitch of her scream reached a level that would shatter every glass in town.

Angel's footsteps pounded on the hardwood floor. "It's okay, Gabby." Reaching their daughter, she scooped her up in a hug.

Sobs replaced the screaming. "Who's that naked man, Mommy?"

Feeling like a complete shit for terrifying his daughter, he wondered if he was even father material. If the past thirty seconds were anything to go by he'd say no. Not only did he fail to comfort Gabriela, he scared her. If she didn't have nightmares before this moment she'd probably have them now.

"He's not naked, Gabby." Angel's intense gaze settled on his chest.

Billy fumbled for his shirt even as he reveled in Angel's appreciative stare, proving that she wasn't immune to him. After waking from a restless sleep on the recliner he'd stripped off the suit jacket, tie and shirt so he could wash up before leaving for his flight home. What was Angel going to say? Would she lie for now? She'd fallen asleep before they had a chance to talk about how to tell Gabriela.

"Sorry, she's not used to having men in the apartment."

He pressed his lips together to keep from smiling. Happy not only for his daughter's sake of not being confused by other 'dads', but that Angel didn't have anyone special in her life. He reminded himself it didn't mean she hadn't found sex elsewhere and the smile he'd been fighting died on his lips. The thought of another man touching her brought out the beast in him.

Angel stroked Gabriela's hair. "Remember when I said your father didn't know about you and I couldn't find him?"

She nodded into Angel's rumpled blouse and mumbled, "You lost him."

"Not exactly lost, but I did find him."

Gabriela cautiously peeked out. God, she was adorable when she wasn't screaming. Dark curls framed her chubby cheeks tinged with a rosy glow. Only the track of her tears marred her angelic face. But those tears he caused still watered in those blue eyes, ready to flow at a moments notice. Billy held his breath, waiting for his daughter—and she was *his* without a doubt—to pass judgment.

Wiping a cheek with a closed fist she asked, "Why do you have hair like a girl?"

Angel laughed.

Billy searched for an explanation suitable for a child. He remembered Angel's fingers threading through its length. Countless women had followed in the years since. His hair had earned him big endorsement deals. "The Mane" as it was dubbed, flowed from the bottom of his helmet making him a household name. That and his lightening speed down the field.

His little girl, however, found him lacking. Wasn't a daughter supposed to think of her dad as a super hero? "Gabriela, do you know the story of Samson from the Bible?"

She nodded, her curls bouncing with the motion.

"She goes to Sunday School," said Angel proudly.

Of course she did. Despite the bar being a place where many an alcoholic or unfaithful spouse passed the time, the O'Malley's were faithful churchgoers. "Well, that's why I keep my hair long."

"Can I braid it?"

"Uh…" That wasn't the reaction he was hoping for. Apparently she wasn't buying the Samson story. Braid his hair? He may wear it in a ponytail from time to time, but a braid? If the guys on the team caught wind of it, he'd never live it down.

"Pleazeeeeee."

She bestowed a smile so stunning he instinctively knew it was some feminine trick she used to get what she wanted. Perhaps he'd catch on to this father gig quicker than he thought. However, knowing you were being played was one thing while actually having a defense against it was another. "Sure."

Angel arched an eyebrow as Gabriela wiggled in her arms.

"Yay! Down, Mommy."

As soon as Gabriela's tiny feet hit the floor, she took his finger into her hand and led him to her room, which he recognized as being Angel's old one. And now, with two beds, he realized it still was. With Gabriela's bed decked out with a purple comforter and gauzy white pillows, it was clear that Angel did her best, but plans to spoil his daughter began to form in his mind.

His gaze zeroed in on the pink elephant settled amongst the other stuffed animals. *Angel kept it?*

Did she ever think about that night? He'd won it for her at the carnival that swooped into town. He spent twenty dollars before knocking down a trio of stacked milk bottles with a baseball but it was well worth the smile he received from the girl everyone referred to as a badass. Later that night they made love for the first time. Maybe fumbled in love would be a more accurate statement.

Now it looked as though the elephant belonged to their daughter. He wondered if Angel had wanted Gabriela to have some small piece of him. Did she hold it at night as she fell asleep? Now his eyes watered as he choked on the emotion flooding into his heart. *What the fuck?* He tucked the feelings away as he sneezed violently. Not tears at all but an allergic reaction to something in the room.

"God bless you," said Angel as she plopped onto her bed for a front row seat.

Gabriela directed him to sit on the floor as she collected a brush and a plastic bin filled with hair accessories. He flinched several times as she yanked the brush through his hair, but he was more focused on her chatter. Angel wasn't kidding when she said Gabby loved to talk. About anything and everything. Flitting from one subject to another so fast that his mind struggled to keep up with her favorite Disney princess, flavor of ice cream, cartoon, and on and on. Hopefully there wasn't a test at the end, if there was an end.

Without taking a breath, she asked. "Do you want one braid or two?"

"One will do," he said. Angel's laughter filled the room. He loved the sound but he had a feeling he was the reason for it. "What's so funny?"

"You look shell-shocked."

"Then I look exactly how I feel." He sneezed again.

A stamp of a tiny foot muffled against the carpet. "Mommy, I need help."

Angel got up and stood behind him. Arousal fired in his blood and he fisted his hands as Angel braided his hair. As a teen he would've pulled her onto to his lap and tickled her until she kissed him. With the familiar feel of her fingers running through his hair, damn if he wasn't tempted to do it now, but his daughter stood by watching her mother's every move.

"See? Now try it again."

Once Gabriela took over, his breathing returned to normal. After several failed attempts, the would-be hairstylist held out two rubber bands in her chubby hand and asked, "Purple or pink?"

Couldn't there be a black one so he could salvage some of his dignity? Judging from the décor of the room it wasn't hard to guess her favorite color. "Purple, of course."

Done she stood in front of him to access her work. "You look silly," she teased. Leaning forward she pressed her nose up against his. "Mommy said my daddy had special eyes just like me."

Billy's shade of cobalt blue needed no touch ups in magazine ads; in fact one would think they used photo manipulation to create the way his gaze leapt off the page. In one of the creepier emails, a fan said she wanted to pluck out his eyeballs and wear them around her neck.

"Mommy said that?" He wanted to ask what else Angel had revealed about him but Angel cleared her throat.

Nodding, Gabriela backed away and tilted her head in deep thought. "Do I call you Daddy?"

Daddy. Such as simple word, but the tug at his heart hurt more than the physical pain of her pulling at his hair. He didn't want to presume or push realizing how delicate this moment was. "Whatever you want."

A mischievous grin grew on her face. "Okay, Poopy-head."

"Gabriela!" Despite the sternness in Angel's voice he caught a hint of a suppressed giggle as mother came around to confront daughter.

Already feeling protective of his little girl he laughed so she wouldn't get in trouble and they both joined in. If anyone had been watching, they'd think they were a real family. He risked saying, "I think I prefer Daddy."

"Good." Gabriela's face grew serious and asked. "Are you going to live with us?"

"I—" Billy's heart leapt but he looked up to Angel for permission. She nodded and Billy continued, "No, I invited you and your Mom to come stay with me."

Gabriela looked up to her mother with wide eyes. "Are you getting married?"

"No!" Angel dropped to her knees. "No, honey." Her tone softened when she took Gabriela's hands in hers. "It's only for a little while and then we'll find a place close to Daddy so you can see him whenever you want."

The way Angel immediately said no like being married to him would be a fate worse than making a living on the pole irked him. On the other hand she generously cleared the way for Gabriela to call him Daddy. Not that he deserved it, but he'd spend the rest of his life earning that honor.

After a long silence Gabriela asked, "Can Lucy come too?"

Lucy? His gut twisted in pain. Could the second bed belong to a child that Angel had with another man? But where were the photos? Gabriela must have noticed his distress mistaking it for an automatic no.

"Pleazzzzzzz… She's so pretty but sometimes Mommy says she needs a time out." Gabriela started to giggle like it was the funniest thing ever.

Now he was really confused. He looked to Angel for answers. "Lucy?"

"Lucifer, is our cat," explained Angel. "Gabby is convinced he is a she."

A cat? Well, that explained the sneezing.

Chapter 6

After an hour of bonding over hair, Billy left the room so she could speak privately to their daughter. Pushing back a curl from Gabby's face, Angel asked one more time, "Are you sure you're okay with moving so far away?"

Gabby nodded. "We have to move anyway. Can I bring my Barbie dolls?"

Angel blinked at her daughter's logic. They had until the end of the month to get out of the apartment and turn over the bar. Tony, who held her father's marker, had the nerve to say he was a good guy by giving her two months to pay up or get out. Even said he'd let her stay if she'd sleep with him. *Yep, a real saint of a pig's ass.*

"Of course you can bring them. But, honey, you probably won't see any of your friends again." Angel worried her daughter didn't understand the full implications of moving to New Jersey.

"I can make new friends. I can't make a daddy. Will he let me eat ice cream?"

"How old are you?" Angel hugged her tightly. Sometimes she swore an old woman lived inside her daughter and at other times she thought Gabby was digressing back into the terrible twos.

Satisfied with her daughter's answers she left Gabby to play in the bedroom and reluctantly joined Billy, who was waiting in the kitchen. He was pouring himself a mug of coffee from a dusty coffee maker that hadn't been used since O'Malley's death two months ago.

"I made you some tea," he said, plopping his big body into a rickety chair, Billy motioned to a chipped mug across from him.

Angel frowned at him as she sat down.

"So you lost me?" He eyed her steadily as he rubbed his thumb back and forth along the handle of his coffee mug.

Ignoring the tea and the fact that he remembered her preference she answered, "I didn't say lost. That's just how Gabby interpreted it. And what was I supposed to say? That you were dead? I wasn't about to tell her that her father preferred to pretend she didn't exist."

"I didn't know she existed."

"So you say now."

Early on she swore she would never tell Gabby the truth. Never. There was a time when she had asked about her father but it stopped eventually. Not unlike how Angel stopped asking about her own mother. O'Malley never talked about it and she learned not to question him for it only brought sadness to his eyes. Is that why Gabby had stopped asking too? Did she see the same haunted look in her mother's eyes when she asked about her daddy? And all this time Angel thought Gabby had forgotten when in reality she'd been hoping for her father to show up.

Truthfully, she'd been betting on a negative reaction from her daughter as an excuse to decline. As they exchanged phone numbers she made one last ditch effort. "The cat is not going to be a problem, is it?" Better he escape now before Gabby became attached.

"No, I'll look into allergy shots." After taking a large gulp of coffee, he asked, "Who names their cat Lucifer?"

"He's a bit of a hellion." Maybe that would get him to rethink his impulsive proposal.

"Ah, a true O'Malley."

"Hey!" Angel instinctively punched him in the arm, like they'd seen each other just yesterday instead of six years ago. They both laughed and for a moment she felt like that teen girl who once fell in love, perhaps because she still was.

No, you're in love with the boy you once knew, the one who won you a pink elephant at a fair. But Billy was no longer that boy. And Angel was definitely no longer that girl. At only twenty-three he had a sexual past that an eighty-year-old man would be proud to remember on his deathbed. *Remember that before you're the one who becomes attached.*

An awkward silence followed the laughter. Then he reached for his wallet and all of the muscles in her body tensed. "No thanks," she said as he tried to hand over a wad of cash.

He opened her clenched fist. "It's just to hold you over until we can settle the legal details and make a permanent arrangement." Placing the money in her palm, he closed her fingers around it. Keeping his hand around hers, he said, "You really don't know the meaning of child support, do you?"

She didn't want his money. Well, she did want a check in the mail every month to help support Gabby. A check didn't send tingles of excitement running from the tips of her fingers, up her arm to surround her heart, or wet her lips down below. His touch, however, did all those things. "I'm not in this to bleed you dry, you know. Once I pass the licensing exam and find a nursing job we'll be fine."

"I hope that we includes me, Angel."

He squeezed her hand, but it was her heart that felt the force of the gesture. She didn't know how to respond because she didn't know exactly what he meant by it. Angel couldn't let the whispered words seduce her into thinking she could be anything more than his baby mama. She winced at the term but in his world that's how she'd be referenced.

Billy released her hand. "My flight leaves in two hours so I better get going."

"One more thing, Billy."

"What's that?"

"To be clear. I will be sleeping in that third bedroom. There'll be no messing around."

"No messing around. Got it."

Angel doubted his rushed agreement, in fact she felt a bit annoyed over it, but she'd hold him to it just the same. Angel walked Billy to the door then called out, "Gabby, come say goodbye."

"No!" Gabby flew down the hall and threw her arms around his leg, which was the size of a small tree trunk. "Don't leave."

Angel's heart clenched at her daughter's desperate plea. Now instead of wishing he'd back out, she decided she would kill him if he did.

Billy picked Gabby up easily as if she were one of his weights at the gym. "It's okay. I'll see you in less than a week."

"You're not gonna get lost again?"

"Never," he promised, kissing her nose. He looked back to Angel and continued, "I'll have my agent send someone to help with the move and make the arrangements."

"Carlos?"

"How do you know my agent?"

You wouldn't know by the expression on his face but whoa, he sounded jealous. Angel was horrified when a secret thrill shot through her. "I called the Cougar team office first and they directed me to your agent. After getting the third degree he refused to put me in touch with you, hence the paternity suit."

Gone was the cool façade and Billy's face hardened into a mask. "That won't happen again."

Angel doubted that but nodded. It would be a new town but the same old story of people trying to keep them apart. "The first priority is getting Gabby registered for school."

"School? Already?"

Gabby held up her fingers. "I'm five. I'm in kindergarten," she said proudly.

"Oh, so you're a big girl," said Billy.

"Only when she wants to be," Angel teased.

He kissed Gabby goodbye and placed her down gently. Angel's heart skipped when his gaze moved from their daughter and seemed to zero in on her lips, but then his eyes met hers and he said, "Don't change your mind."

The door closed and in relief her heartbeat steadied. But as she heard his footfalls on the steps, disappointment replaced relief. The back door opened and closed. It felt like she hadn't had air since he strode into the bar last night. She took a cleansing breath before gazing down at her daughter who swung her body back and forth looking up at her mother expectantly. "So what do you think of your Daddy?"

On her tippy toes, with her hand reaching up into the air, Gabby said, "He's a giant." Spinning on one foot, she turned. With arms now stretched wide, she stomped down the hallway to her room, taking such big steps that she was almost leaping. "Fee, fie, fo, fum."

Billy had earned major brownie points for letting Gabby tug on his hair until Angel thought he'd end up bald. But a morning of playtime did not a father make.

How would he deal with the messes? The constant questions? When Gabby woke with a stomachache? Then again who would've thought she herself had an ounce of maternal instinct? Certainly not Angel. Yet as soon as Gabriela was placed in her arms, a mother bear mentality rooted itself deep within her.

An hour later a knock sounded. She guessed it was Hoss and even though she didn't want a confrontation she wanted to get it over with and opened the door.

"You let him sleep over."

"Shhh," she said as she pointed down the hall to where Gabby was napping unusually early. Between the sleepover and the excitement of meeting her father she had volunteered to take a nap. A first. Angel took a seat on the couch as Hoss softly closed the door. "It's not what you think." Angel explained what O'Malley' had done and about Billy's offer to move to New Jersey. "Why would O'Malley lie to me?"

"I don't know." Hoss plopped down onto O'Malley's chair.

"Why did he make me break up with him in the first place? Why wasn't I good enough?" It was a question she had on the tip of her tongue for years and now finally she was able to ask it out loud.

"Jesus, Angel, is that what you thought?"

"O'Malley told me so right to my face." It only confirmed what the whole town thought of her. Even Carlos, a man she'd never met, thought she was a gold digger. In his agent's defense, allegations were probably made against his clients everyday. How many claims did Billy himself receive—hell did he actually have other kids?

"He didn't mean it. He knew Billy would break your heart. Your father wanted you to walk away with your pride."

"Billy wouldn't break—"

"He would have eventually. College women throwing themselves at him versus a pool hustler five hundred miles away? Not even a contest. It's a given."

"I'll never truly know, will I?" Angel folded her arms.

Hoss flipped back the recliner and sighed. "Don't start believing in those fairy tales you read to Gabby. Nothing has changed. Replay that video of him in the strip club. That's the real Billy Burner not the boy who whispered promises to you in the dark. Remember that when he tries to get you into bed. Don't think he won't. He's a man."

"And the father of my child."

"A sperm donor."

But Billy claimed to want more and by the way he melted when he looked at Gabby, she already had him wrapped around her finger.

"When are you leaving?" Hoss got up and walked to the door.

"Next week."

Hoss hesitated, and Angel thought he was about to offer up some more unwanted fatherly advice but instead asked, "Can I have the chair?"

Angel blinked. What was she going to do with all this stuff? She doubted any of it was worth the cost of moving to New Jersey or the cost to store it once it got there. Besides she deserved a clean slate without reminders of the past. Like how much O'Malley loved that chair, joking that he'd be buried in it. Now as far as she was concerned, he could roll in his grave knowing Hoss sat on the O'Malley throne. "Consider it severance."

"Ha, good one. I'll come by with a truck later."

Angel shut the door. Leaning against it in exhaustion, she decided to allow herself the rest of the day to brood about the past. Then tomorrow she'd start anew. Begin to pack up her life and get the hell out of town before she changed her mind. Or Billy changed his.

Chapter 7

After practice Billy stood on the sidelines of the empty field, visualizing the plays for tomorrow's game. In his head he ran every route, pictured catching each pass with ease before making his move to score a touchdown or dig for that extra yard. He'd repeat the process tonight as he fell asleep, when he woke, and one more time before he took the field. The ritual began in college when the step up from high school football had overwhelmed him. Skill wasn't enough at that level. He realized to be a successful player he had to be prepared physically and mentally. He welcomed the challenge.

Concentrating on football was the only thing that had kept him sane in those first few months after Angel dumped him. Billy poured his pain into practices, played like an animal in games, earning him the college scholarship his father always dreamed of.

He breathed in the calming smell of grass and closed his eyes enjoying the peace of the moment before heading to the madness of the locker room. There was so much to do before Angel and Gabriela arrived on Wednesday. There was no room for a game ending fumble.

Ryan Terell, the veteran tight end, slapped Billy's shoulder pad. "Daydreaming about breaking my records, kid?"

Billy shrugged it off. "I'm not a kid."

Jake Miller, the running back, slapped the other side. "So we've heard."

Billy should have known. Where there was one, the other was sure to follow. The two hated him and seemed to live to ride his ass for every misstep. He knew he'd stepped out of bounds when he asked out both of their women, but in his defense if his teammates couldn't close the deal then it should have been every man for himself. Football is a team sport, but sex was a one-on-one game. "Coach has a big mouth."

Terell shook his head. "We share agents."

Billy had warned Carlos not to interfere again. He'd fire the prick, but he was the rare combination of genius and shark. His clients received the best contracts and the most lucrative endorsements. The man even plotted out the future, for life after football, which no player could conceive of while playing. Call it a superstition, call it ego, or maybe a little of both.

Since his teammates knew about his daughter, Billy better get around to telling his father. He dreaded the conversation knowing his father would blow up. Even as a man Billy still tried to please him. Why? Habit? The easy way out? It was something he needed to examine. Dating Angel had pissed off his father and it was the first time and last time they'd ever gone head-to-head. Angel only proved his father right by tearing out his heart.

But now grandpa would just have to deal with it. Hell, if Gabriela couldn't melt his father's steel-dipped heart, then there was no hope for the man. Regardless, Billy wasn't going anywhere and planned to be a major part of Gabriela's life.

"Did you get a DNA test?" asked Miller.

Billy fisted his hands, fighting the instinct to punch Miller in the mouth. He shot back a retort instead, "Did you ask Hannah for one? If I remember, you two split for a while last year." He knew the comment would drive Miller crazy, since Billy had asked out the supermodel at the time.

Miller pointed a finger at him. "If we weren't team-mates I'd be scraping what's left of you off of my cleats." Miller stormed off to the locker room.

Billy laughed it off, but his humor quickly faded when Terell gripped him by the jersey and tugged him forward.

"You're an asshole," said Terell. "You're not a rookie anymore. Grow the fuck up."

Before Billy could reply with an insincere apology, Terell pulled at Billy's jersey again. "We're only looking out for you." The frustration on Terell's face was not an act.

Holy crap. Terell wasn't kidding. Billy had been so busy trying to prove himself an asset to the team that maybe he hadn't realized Terell had been trying to mentor him all along. Perhaps all those perceived digs about his play had actually been constructive criticism. Stunned by the truth, Billy decided to chuck the chip on his shoulder and his bad boy ways for the good of the team and for the sake of his daughter. "Sorry, man."

Terell let go of his jersey and gave him a light shove. "It's not me you need to apologize to."

"Yeah, I'll get on it." Billy turned to go and Terell followed.

"Burner, watch out for Marcus tomorrow. He hits hard."

The Texas Stars lineman was feared throughout the league but Billy never showed fear and normally Terell didn't either, which was a bad sign for his teammate. Had Terell lost his edge? Is that why he had announced his retirement after the upcoming season? "He's gotta catch me first."

"You know Marcus is not going to be the only one to enjoy seeing that smirk of yours pounded into the turf on Sunday."

Billy might not be afraid of going one on one on the field against Marcus but as he approached Miller in the locker room his insides shook. "Look man, I—"

"Forgotten." Miller and Burner bumped fists. "Hopefully your kid doesn't look like you."

Relieved, Billy laughed and then shook his head. "Looks like her mother, except for the eyes." And why he didn't need a DNA test. This unspoken truth lay between them, as did the awkward silence, which seem to drown out the shouts of the other players and music blaring in the background.

Miller finally nodded. "Good, cause you're an ugly mother fucker."

Two days later the doorbell rang just as Billy put ice on his shoulder, which took the brunt of the Star's attempt to see him dead. As much as it hurt, the fact that the other team sent their best defensive player after him meant they considered him a real threat. The loss pained him more, even if it was only a preseason game.

Not expecting company, he peered through the peep-hole. Miller, Terell, and their wives stood waiting. Opening the door he noticed the paint cans, painting supplies and Jake and Hannah's baby girl. "What's this all about?"

"Everything happened so fast, we figured you didn't have time to decorate," explained Samantha, Terell's wife, a former journalist who almost ruined his life when she thought he was taking steroids. She was not only smart, but clever too. Add her pretty face and nice rack and it equaled a dangerous combination that had brought Terell to his knees.

Feeling scrutinized under her gaze, he pulled at his collar in discomfort. He had propositioned both of these women and the awkwardness of them standing with his teammates shamed him. "But why would you help me?"

"Because we're family, fuck face." Terell handed him a paintbrush. "Lead the way."

Billy smiled as he guided them down the hallway. It was obvious this wasn't his teammates idea. He loved witnessing them being led by the balls by their wives. He opened the door. "This will be Gabriela's room."

"You expect a little girl to feel at home in this squalor?" Hannah shook her head. From her tone and expression you'd think the place swarmed with cockroaches.

Billy looked at the white walls and double bed covered in a beige comforter. Simple, yes. Squalor, no. "I ordered some girly stuff on-line. It'll be here before they move in," he defended. Okay, so the room wouldn't be exactly Disney World inspired but he'd have it all purpled up before Gabby slept one night in it.

"Speaking of they, where will the mother of your child sleep?" Hannah asked.

Mother of his child? Did Hannah have to say it that way, as if Angel was a saint instead of having a body created for sin? Leaving Miller and Terell to open the paint cans, they crossed the hallway to the third bedroom.

"Is she supposed to sleep on the weight bench?" Hannah Hahn's special talent wasn't modeling. It was laying men low. Between the tone of her voice and her condescending look, Billy's stomach roiled in embarrassment.

The dressing down he'd gotten for hitting on her still stung to this day. He wondered how Miller's huge ego withstood her diva act. Beauty only went so far in his book. Still, he found the way the baby snuggled close to her endearing. He crossed his arms to fill the void he felt from missing this part of Gabriela's life.

Strewn about the room, his gym equipment took up most of the space. "I was going to move it out."

"No, you weren't. You were hoping to talk her into your bed," said Samantha.

He wasn't about to confess his foolish teenage love for Angel or how even now he hoped to convince her to make a go of it. They wouldn't believe him anyway. Let them think he was a jerk. "And?"

"Honey, Burner needs help moving this stuff out," Hannah yelled.

The ladies left the room as Miller came in. With raised brows and a head nod to the bandage on Billy's arm, he asked, "You juicing?"

"Allergy shots. The kid has a cat." He was damn sick of being accused and tested for steroids. Most athletes had their favorite charities and Billy was no different. His foundation educated student athletes on the hazards of performance enhancing drugs. A lesson he wished his friend had learned before dropping dead of a heart attack at the age of twenty.

"Aww, the things we fathers will do for our little girls."

"True that. I let her braid my hair," admitted Billy.

Miller burst out laughing. Rubbing the bald head that Hannah seemed so fond of, Miller said, "Don't have to worry about that."

Surrounded by the support of his teammates, Billy's nerves dissipated. At Angel's apartment he'd been out of his element, but from here on out he would have the home field advantage.

Chapter 8

The sheer terror of what lay ahead had distracted Angel from her fear of flying. The fact that the owner of the NY Cougars had sent his private jet only added to her distress. How many other people knew about Billy's illegitimate daughter? How many would think Angel was nothing but a gold digger. The thought they'd become tabloid fodder crossed her mind more than once. But this hardly could be news, right? In fact, it was more par for the course with athletes. As long as they left her daughter out of it, she didn't care.

Gabby's innocent excitement had bubbled over into constant chatter for the entire length of the flight. Now she slept in a coma like state in the back of the limo as it pulled out of Newark Airport and headed towards Billy's apartment along the Hudson River. Angel's nerves wound tighter and tighter as they passed each mile marker. Was she doing the right thing? Her stomach roiled with hunger. She popped a few of Gabby's Goldfish crackers into her mouth to stave off the pangs. The food offered by the beautiful flight attendant may have been a gourmet leap from regular airline fare, but it had held no appeal at the time.

Speaking of beautiful, Angel's gaze landed on Lanie, Carlos' efficient assistant, who sat across from her in the limo. When Billy had said Carlos would send someone to lend a hand, she hadn't counted on a spy as well. That was a little harsh. The woman had gone out of her way to help with the move and patiently answered Gabby's endless questioning. Actually Angel thought her daughter the better spy.

Lanie looked up from her notes and smiled. Angel tried to reciprocate, but for the millionth time she wondered if Billy and Lanie had ever dated. With long blonde hair and sleek legs, the former model fit his typical hookup. In other words she was everything Angel wasn't.

"I didn't sleep with him," Lanie stated.

"I didn't—."

"Yes, you did. Don't worry I'm used to people assuming I slept with Carlos' client list."

Knowing exactly how that felt, Angel warmed to Lanie instantly. "Do you like working for Carlos?" It wouldn't hurt to learn more about the man who might try to come between her and Billy.

"He's tough as nails, but he truly cares about his clients."

"Which is why you've been sizing me up this whole time."

"Touché."

"And what will your report say?" Angel looked out the window as the limo raced down the highway.

"That you two were a Bon Jovi song in the making," said Lanie.

"Darn, I thought of us as Romeo and Juliet."

"Girl, you're in Jersey now."

"For better or worse." Angel looked back to Lanie and smiled for the first time that day, even if it was more of a nervous smile than a genuine one. She liked Lanie, especially since now she knew the woman hadn't slept with Billy.

Lanie lifted a brow. "Strange choice of words."

For better or worse. Was it a Freudian slip? Would it be something she reported back to Carlos? Or worse, to Billy? "I didn't mean—"

"Relax, I'm kidding. You're wound tighter than my face after Botox."

The limo pulled up to a soaring apartment building. The sun glinted off the façade's blue and green glass. Angel woke up a grumpy Gabby, but as they got out of the limo, Gabby spotted Billy walking towards them and brightened with wide eyes and a smile. "Daddy!" Squirming out of Angel's grip, she ran to him.

Billy swooped her up. "Don't you look pretty."

Nervous over, well, everything, Angel blurted, "It's new, she picked it out herself. I used the money you gave me." That it took over an hour for Gabby to decide on the yellow dress, Angel left out. She feared she had a fashionista on her hands.

"Angel, you don't have to explain how you spent the money."

"Doesn't Mommy look pretty too?"

"Gabby." Angel smoothed out the nonexistent wrinkles. The black Rayon/nylon spandex combination lived up to its promises as the perfect travel dress. The cut hugged her curves, showing a not-so-respectful amount of cleavage. And while not in mommy dress mode neither was she runway ready. Unlike Lanie, who wore a chic tan skirt, an emerald green blouse, and Jimmy Choo slingbacks.

But by the way Billy's gaze traveled from Angel's red polished toenails, which peeked out from practical heeled sandals, and all the way up to her favorite purple lipstick, she might as well have been naked. His intense gaze finally reached her eyes and he said, "Very pretty."

She tried not to read too much into the words, but the story his eyes told filled her with a longing to match his own.

"Whoa. Do you want me to babysit while you two get 'reacquainted'?" asked Lanie.

So Angel wasn't the only one who felt the heat radiating between them. It only took a spark to set off their volatile attraction. Lust easily sated, but love a puzzle with missing pieces. "That won't be necessary," said Angel in a flat tone.

Billy returned his attention back to Gabby. "I live all the way up there." Pointing way up, he asked, "What do you think?"

Gabby tilted her head back until she was almost arching her spine in Billy's arms in order to take in the towering building. "It looks like the Emerald City Castle."

It kind of did, admitted Angel. She smiled, loving her daughter's active imagination and then looked to Billy and said, "That's from the Wizard of Oz."

"I'm not completely clueless," said Billy in a tight whisper. The driver deposited the pet carrier at his feet and Lucifer meowed loudly.

Billy carried Gabby and the cat's cage while two porters from the building appeared to help with the luggage. Lanie waved goodbye as the limo pulled away. "Good luck."

Luck? If Angel had any hope of keeping her heart safe, she needed a miracle. Coming through the revolving door, Angel tried to appear unaffected by the elegant lobby. A chandelier the size of a car hung from the ceiling. White marble floor tiles sparkled underneath its glow. With a slight upwards tilt of her chin, she did her best Audrey Hepburn impression and glided to the elevator. Gabby talked non-stop all the way up, and Billy merely nodded, smiling like a new daddy, which she supposed he sort of was.

Finally at the top, Billy opened the door to the apartment and placed Gabby down. She rushed in to explore. Hesitant, Angel waited until the workers placed the luggage inside and left smiling with a large tip in their hands. Taking a deep breath, she ventured into Billy's lair. Only it wasn't the playboy bachelor pad she assumed he would have; it wasn't even frat boy inspired. Oh sure there was the leather sofa, but everything else exuded a clean sophistication. So much so she wondered if this unit had been a model to sell other units in the building and Billy purchased as is. Compared to her apartment back home, this was a palace.

Gabby ran to the horseshoe shaped couch, jumped up, and ran across the cushions while giggling.

"Gabriela!"

"It's okay," said Billy, a big smile on his face.

"It's not okay. She knows better." Angel dug her nails into the palms of her hands. They weren't in his apartment two minutes and Billy was already trying to undermine her authority.

"I want her to feel at home. Both of you."

"And you think I let her jump on the furniture?"

"Uh, no...I," Billy stammered.

"Just because my couch wasn't good enough for the Salvation Army doesn't mean I allowed Gabby to jump on it."

Before Billy could respond, Gabby diffused her mother's anger by saying, "That's what beds are for. Right, Mommy?"

Angel mentally counted to ten. On occasion she had let Gabby jump on her bed. "Right," said Angel, her voice calm once again.

"Can I see my room?"

"You sure can." Billy picked up the crate and Lucy hissed his displeasure. Seemingly unfazed Billy escorted Gabby to her new room.

Squeals of delight sprung from her daughter's mouth while Angel's jaw dropped in shock. A light shade of pink graced the walls. The furniture included a white dresser with purple polka dots and a kid sized table and chairs with a tea service already set up. The high double bed, which alone would've been a step up from the twin Gabby woke up in this morning, could only be described as a bed fit for a fairy princess. The oversized lavender comforter created the effect of cotton candy and any kid, hell any adult, would want to dive right in. As if that wasn't enough, a canopy of white gossamer with tiny white lights woven through the fabric pooled to the floor. How much did this cost? And moments ago Angel had agreed that beds were made for jumping. Not this bed. Oh no.

Gabby vaulted herself onto the bed, almost lost in a cloud of purple. "This is the bestest room ever. Isn't it, Mommy?"

Torn between the wide-eyed happiness of her daughter and anger at Billy for the over-the-top extravagance, she bit her lip before she said something petty. Gabby might never want to leave this purple paradise. Was that Billy's plan? Deep inside she fumed, but for now she put on her happy face. "Yes, it's the bestest," she agreed.

Gabby stopped and looked around. "Is Mommy sleeping in your room?" she asked her father.

A moment of panic relit Angel's nerves before remembering there was supposed to be a third bedroom. Gabby had it in her head that they were going to be a family. Angel should press about finding her own apartment as soon as possible. By the way father and daughter bonded, it wouldn't take long for them to be comfortable without Angel around. To train Billy in the basics of caring for a five-year-old might take a bit longer. Still, she had to think of Gabby's emotional health as well. With living in a new state, new living arrangements, new school, and hell, a new daddy, Angel would have to play it by ear.

"No, her room is right across the hall. Why don't you play in here while I show Mommy her new room."

"Can I let Lucy out now?"

"Sure," agreed Billy.

"God help us all. Gabby keep him in your room for now until he's not so mad anymore."

"Is he dangerous?"

Angel thought him sweet for protecting his daughter, but she couldn't help teasing him about his overreaction. "Geez, he's a housecat not a tiger."

They crossed the hall and Billy opened the door, but he let Angel walk in first. From the vanity table to the ruby red comforter on the double bed, everything spoke of old Hollywood glamour. Now she really felt like she was in an Audrey Hepburn movie. How had he pulled this off? She was worried about Gabby never wanting to leave and now she was having the same thoughts herself.

"Don't get too comfortable."

Angel blinked at the hurtful words. Had he read her thoughts? "You don't have to remind me. I'll start looking for a place tomorrow."

"That's not what I meant." Billy backed her up against the footboard. "I want you in my bed."

But for how long? Angel's voice caught in her throat. Then he stroked her cheek, and in a panic she rushed out, "Billy, we agreed, no messing around." There was nowhere to run but the bed and that was a bad idea. Very bad. Very naughty. Oh, hell.

"I'm not messing around." His fingers brushed along her neck. "I'm totally serious."

Her pulse leapt under his touch. One part of her wanted to flee and another part wanted to melt into his embrace. Their gazes locked. His vivid blue eyes mirrored her want. It had taken him only minutes to wear down her defenses. Billy was going to kiss her and she was going to let him. Let him? Hell, if he didn't get to it, she'd kiss him.

Her gaze dropped to his lips and on cue, he dipped his head. Just one more breath away and she'd feel again.

"What are you doing?" asked Gabby.

Chapter 9

Blocked by a five-year-old. Billy hung his head in defeat. He'd been so close to showing Angel what she'd missed these last six years. So close to finding out if the reality lived up to the memory of those heavenly lips on his.

It would have to wait. The way he wanted to kiss Angel should not be witnessed by anyone under the age of eighteen. Hell, an adult would learn a thing or two. Still he wasn't going to lie to Gabriela. Lifting his head, he stared directly into Angel's cat-like green eyes. "I was about to kiss Mommy."

Angel's eyes widened, and he heard Gabriela giggle. Pleased by both reactions, he backed away turning his attention to his daughter. "What's the matter, sweetie?"

"Lucy pooped on the floor." Her hand flew to her mouth in an attempt to hold back a giggle.

Was she laughing because she said the word poop? He smiled, not even caring about the mess on the carpet. His daughter already had him wrapped around her pinkie finger. Hopefully she'd never figure that out.

"Where's the litter box?" Angel asked.

Billy looked to the ceiling. He thought he'd covered everything. Rooms decorated, check. Groceries purchased, check. Safety locks on the balcony door, check.

"You did buy a litter box, didn't you?" prodded Angel.

"It wasn't on the list."

"Neither was the rags-to-riches princess room or this," she said tightly. Angel waved her hand around her bedroom.

"I wanted you both to feel welcomed here. Wanted." Ah, hell, why were tears welling up in Angel's eyes? "What did I do wrong now?"

Angel collapsed onto the bed. "Nothing. I'm sorry. You've been like a knight in shining armor, and I've been the wicked witch of the Mid West."

Gabriela ran over to her mother and patted her head. "You're not a witch, Mommy."

Billy agreed. Angel might be an enchantress but she was no witch. And him a knight in shining armor? Billy rubbed his neck, uncomfortable with the comparison. As his daughter he wanted Gabriela to have the best, nothing heroic about that. He was hoping to impress Angel, not alienate her. He looked around the room and pictured Gabriela's room in his head. "I guess I did go overboard," he conceded.

"No, it's not you, it's me," said Angel.

"Where have I heard that before?" he muttered, but by the intake of her breath he guessed she heard it just the same. He was a fool to believe anything had changed. "I'll run out to the store."

"Billy—"

Before she could finish he was out the door. He didn't want to hear it.

By the time he returned, it was time to get Gabriela ready for bed and Angel efficiently went over their daughter's bedtime routine with him.

Once they had Gabriela snuggled into bed, Angel read from The Princess and the Pea while he leaned against the bedpost and watched. The soft glow of the fairy lights draping down the canopy created a magical scene. Mesmerized by the way the words flowed from Angel's lips, Billy only half listened to the tale as his body reacted from fantasies of its own.

"Kiss Ellie goodnight." Gabriela waved the pink elephant in the air.

Startled by the intrusion and a bit ashamed by his thoughts, he waited until Angel kissed the stuff animal and then Gabriela. He wanted to ask about the elephant, but then Gabriela, waved it in his direction.

"Daddy's turn."

How ridiculous did a hulking football player look kissing a pink elephant? He didn't give it a second thought and complied. His daughter's smile melted his heart. As she hugged the stuffed animal, he kissed her on the cheek, regretting all the goodnight kisses he'd missed.

Angel nodded towards the door. Once they were in the hallway, she touched his arm. "I'm sorry about earlier."

Billy looked down at the hand on his bicep. He flexed the muscle.

"Oh," she gasped.

"What are you exactly sorry about?" He stepped closer, brushing his fingers along her cheek. "Being interrupted?"

"Yes, I mean, no." Angel backed away.

But he persisted, backing her up against the closed door of her room. His fingers threaded through her long black hair. "Do you remember the first time we kissed?"

"No, I mean, yes."

Billy captured her breathless whisper in a gentle kiss. Her lips tasted like heaven and sugar. Angel's hands rested unsure upon his chest as if ready to ward him off, and then they slid around his body as she melted into him. His body hardened. His blood raged for more, but still he kept the kiss soft, unwilling to ruin the sweetness of the moment.

He had a choice. Play the short game for instant gratification or the long game for the win. The long game took patience and that was a game strategy Billy had never excelled at, but to win Angel, he'd learn some new moves. He pulled away. Looking into her eyes he read the emotion there and knew he made the right call. *Trust.*

"Goodnight, Angel."

Walking into his bedroom he realized it was only nine. Unless he wanted to run into Angel and test his new found patience, he was in a prison of his own making. At least he had cable.

Billy spent a restless night tossing and turning. If he wasn't worrying about Gabriela's first night sleeping alone then he was thinking about Angel under the covers just one door away. The alarm sounded and he groaned. Time to get ready for another brutal day of practice. Damn, he'd be a worthless sack of shit on the field. He made his way to the kitchen passing by both rooms as quietly as a 6'5", 250 pound man could possibly be expected to be.

Opening the fridge, he took out all the makings for a fruit smoothie. After throwing them haphazardly into the blender, he pulsed it on low, hoping he wouldn't wake either of the ladies of the house. Needing a blast of energy, he gulped directly from the blender's pitcher. Before finishing it, he decided to start the oatmeal. His body needed fuel for the day ahead.

"Hi."

If the voice hadn't been so small, Billy might have been startled since he hadn't heard the little ninja's footsteps. He turned around and his daughter stood right behind him. She looked up at him with wide eyes, her hair an unruly mass of curls. "Good morning, Gabriela."

She frowned at him, her face so serious he thought she might cry. What had he done wrong? The urge to wake Angel had him eying the hallway. He stared down bigger men every day on the field, yet he was afraid to be alone with a five-year-old.

"Are you mad at me?"

Billy blinked. "No." He hadn't yelled or even scowled at her. "Why do you think that?"

"Mommy only calls me Gabriela when I'm in trouble."

Amused, he asked, "Are you in trouble often?"

"Oh, no." she shook her head vehemently, her ebony curls bouncing in all directions.

Billy laughed. Damn, she had to be the most adorable child that ever lived. She continued to stare up at him. *Now what?* He eyed the hallway again. *Man up, Billy or rather Dad up.* "Are you hungry?"

Gabriela nodded. "Can I have ice cream?"

Billy grinned. "I know I'm pretty new at this dad stuff, but even I know ice cream is not for breakfast."

She pointed to his glass. "Then what's that?"

He guessed his smoothie did look like a milkshake. Observant child. He better remember that in the future. "It's a fruit smoothie. Do you want to try it?"

"Yes, please."

Sorting through his glassware, he selected a mug she'd be able to hold with ease. He transferred a small amount of the liquid and handed her the mug. She took a tentative sip.

"Yum. It taste like a milkshake!"

Overly proud of himself for such a minor achievement, Billy smiled. "Do you want me to make you one?"

"Yes, please."

His daughter watched his every move as he put all the ingredients in the blender, which made him nervous, which was ridiculous. He substituted yogurt for his normal scoop of protein powder and flipped the switch. Her hands flew up to her ears as the ingredients mixed together. Once it was done he filled the mug to the rim. "Here you go, Gabby."

Billy didn't know if the wide smile he received from her was for the smoothie or from the use of her nickname. It didn't matter why, only that he made her happy and damn if he wouldn't do anything in his power to see that smile again and again.

"Thank you." She went to take a sip, but then asked, "Do you have a straw?"

He didn't and he wished he could run out to the store and buy some. "No, I don't, sorry."

"That's okay."

Billy breathed a sigh of relief. He made his oatmeal while Gabby happily sipped her breakfast. He hoped he'd done the right thing. Angel hadn't gone over Gabby's meal schedule, so he had no idea what she normally ate for breakfast. Well, one time couldn't hurt and a fruit smoothie was healthier than those sugar-laced cereals.

Billy noted the time on the oven clock. "Should we wake Mommy up with breakfast in bed?"

Gabby nodded with excitement.

Using a baking pan as a makeshift bed tray, Billy placed a cup of tea and a buttered muffin on it and let Gabby lead the way. He couldn't say who was more surprised, Angel who gushed over the simple fare or him as he salivated over her nipples which puckered underneath the thin, white tank top. What else lay beneath the covers? He instantly regretted his decision last night to be patient. He'd give a whole new meaning to breakfast in bed by feasting on her. "I have to leave for practice but I already made Gabby breakfast."

"I had a milk shake," said Gabby. She climbed onto the bed to sit next to her mother.

Angel's annoyed gaze landed on her prey. The mama bear stare was fiercer than any defense he'd played against, he held up his hands in mock surrender before she launched into another tirade. "A fruit smoothie," he explained. "I swear."

Chapter 10

"Gabrielaaaa…" Angel stretched out her daughter's name in a shocked tone that prompted an explanation of Gabby's white lie.

Gabby shrugged. "It tastes like one."

Billy laughed. Angel breathed a sigh of relief. He wasn't mad that she had jumped to conclusions. Hadn't she learned anything from her little outburst last night? The poor man probably didn't know what hit him. Here he was trying to do the right thing and she jumped all over him—and not in the jump-your-bones good kind of way that kept her up most of the night wondering what would've have happened if the gentle kiss led to more.

"Lanie will be here around ten to show you Gabby's new school. Then to the bank to set up an account for you and a college fund for Gabby."

Would their daughter like her new school? Would she make new friends? Worried for Gabby she only managed to mutter, "Okay, thanks."

Guilt etched his features. "Look I'm sorry. I'd take you myself, but I have practice."

"I understand. Really."

Billy nodded before bending down to kiss Gabby goodbye on the cheek.

"Now kiss mommy." Gabby giggled.

Where did that come from? Angel turned her head. "Daddy isn't—"

Instead of catching a cheek, which Billy must've been aiming for, his lips grazed hers. Stunned, she didn't finish whatever it was she was about to say. Billy leaned back but still remained only a breath away, his blue eyes searching hers. What did he see? Shock? Panic? Desire? All those feelings whirled inside her.

"Yay!" Gabby clapped.

She needed to have another talk with Gabby to remind her that Mommy and Daddy were just friends. But with her lips still tingling from Billy's soft kiss, Angel couldn't form a coherent sentence. It was just as well since she didn't trust herself to speak. He backed away with a smile that promised a more thorough exploration of her lips.

Hell, Angel needed another talk with herself before she started believing Billy really was a knight in shining armor or her very own Prince Charming. Yeah, a real prince all right, one who took his date to a strip joint. But it was becoming increasingly difficult to reconcile the man in the videos with the teenage boy she remembered and the man she was coming to know now.

With Billy finally out of her bedroom, she could convince herself he was simply a man. A gorgeous hunk of a man, but still a man, and men were selfish creatures designed only to satisfy themselves.

Later that afternoon Angel collapsed onto the couch, not so much physically exhausted as mentally and emotionally worn out. Her worries over Gabby liking her new school were unfounded. Her little one was handling this so much better than her mommy. The amount of money Billy wired to Angel's new account astounded her. Lanie explained it was for back child support. The legal details would be hammered out later, which only reminded Angel that playing house with Billy had a closing date. With the cash she could move out anytime she wanted and while Gabby napped she planned to scour the Internet for apartments. Once she was settled she could begin researching the nursing license process for New Jersey. Thankfully, for right now, Billy had given her the gift of time.

She got up to fix a cup of tea and before she could take a calming sip the doorbell sounded. Wasn't the doorman supposed to buzz the intercom before letting people up? Maybe, it was a neighbor.

She peered through the peephole. Two beautiful women stood in the hall. The brunette held a bottle of wine and the tall blonde held an infant of about three months. Oh, hell was the baby his? A sick, sinking feeling clawed inside her stomach. Then she recognized the blonde as the supermodel Hannah Hahn who'd married one of Billy's teammates but who was the other one? A girlfriend of Billy's?

The doorbell buzzed again. Looking down, she compared the worn jeans and faded t-shirt she wore to the women's designer versions of the same attire. There was nothing she could do about it now. She squared her shoulders, refusing to be intimidated by a supermodel and whoever the brunette was.

With the fake, happy waitress smile she perfected over the years she opened the door. "Billy's not here."

"Of course he isn't," said the supermodel, breezing by Angel into the living room. "Our husbands are at practice."

"We're the welcoming committee." The brunette waved the bottle of wine in the air and followed Hannah in. "I'm Samantha Jameson, Ryan Terell's wife. And that," she pointed to the other woman, "Is Hannah Hahn, Jake Miller's wife and her little one is Maxine."

She didn't recognize Samantha Jameson, but Angel knew the name. She wasn't prepared to entertain an award-winning journalist or the supermodel.

And how should Angel introduce herself? As Billy's former lover? Baby mama? She simply settled on, "I'm Angel." She decided to let them draw their own conclusions.

Gabby ran to greet the visitors, apparently awaken by the commotion or perhaps she'd never been asleep at all. She had to admit her baby was growing up. After all as her daughter argued earlier 'kindergarteners do not take naps'.

While the two women fussed over Gabby, Angel escaped to the kitchen to open the wine. And guzzle a glass before facing them again, to hell with the tea. She couldn't find the wineglasses, which made her insanely happy. No wine glasses, no women. The utensil she used was more of a bottle opener than a corkscrew. Luckily Billy had a well-stocked fridge so she could offer cheese and sliced apples to go along with the wine, though a nice serving platter wasn't to be had either. So she made due with a dinner plate and beer mugs. All those years of waitressing at O'Malley's paid off as she balanced the items like a pro. Taking a deep breath she headed for the living room. "Sorry, I don't know where Billy keeps the good china."

"Oh, honey, I'm sure he doesn't have any," said Hannah.

Angel burst out laughing and the two women joined in.

"What's so funny?" Gabby asked.

Hannah and Samantha filled Angel's head with gossip until her head spun with names and events. She looked down at her mug. *Empty. Oh, hell.* She hoped they didn't think she was a lush. Despite practically downing the wine Angel remained silent. What could she say to Hannah, a Supermodel and Samantha, a famous journalist turned author with a controversial bestseller about her time in Iraq? What possibly could a barmaid and pool hustler have in common with them? How could she ever compete?

Yeah, but I can save a life. Could save a life. Would, once she started working as an ER nurse. Still, knowing Samantha's husband was Billy's main competition for the number one tight end spot left her uncomfortable. Angel didn't know what to think. She expected the third degree from the two wives but they didn't pry at all.

"Excuse me, I have to go to the bathroom now," stated Gabby.

"She is a very polite child," said Samantha when Gabby left the room.

"We're working on it." She'd had to remind Gabby not to announce to the world when she needed to use the restroom. *Geez.*

"She's adorable. Billy is so proud of her," said Hannah. "And I think he still carries a torch for her mother."

"Hannah…" Samantha said as a warning.

"What? We women have to stick together. Besides if we left it up to Billy he'd just screw it up."

Angel played it down. "There's nothing to screw up. This is just temporary. I'll be looking for an apartment for us once Billy is comfortable with overnight visits."

"Honey, he may have lured you here with that nonsense, but he wants a second chance," Hannah said.

So much for not prying. Apparently their curiosity was only lying in wait until Gabby left the room. "It's not a matter of a second chance." *Gabby, hurry up and get back in here. Save me.* "Truthfully, I broke it off with him, so I'd be the one asking for a second chance."

"Well that explains a lot," Samantha said.

"Explains what?" asked Angel.

"It's not important." Hannah threw a death glare at Samantha.

"Hit on both of you, didn't he?" she guessed. Both women remained silent, answering her question. She nodded her acceptance of this fact. She wasn't even surprised. Of course he did, they were beautiful women.

"Angel, it was a long time ago before we were married," explained Samantha.

"And nothing happened," added Hannah. "Billy is what I call a Lost Boy."

"They are all Lost Boys until they meet the right woman," said Samantha.

"True," said Hannah. "Now that we got THAT awkwardness out of the way we can concentrate on being friends."

Friends? That would be nice, really nice, but Angel was only living here as a temporary solution. She wasn't a wife, she wasn't even a girlfriend. Once she moved out, she'd have no reason to be associated with anyone from the team.

"And you and Billy can focus on the here and now," suggested Hannah.

"But we're not the same people who fell in love."

Samantha held up the mug, gazing into the red liquid. "Do we really change much from who we are as teenagers? We may be older, wiser, and bring our past hurts along with us, but essentially we are either trying to relive our youth or heal our wounds from them."

Ouch, but that did hit home. Angel had hurt Billy exactly where it would hurt the most. Billy hadn't believed she'd break up with him over Vegas. So she lied, telling him she faked it. How careless she had been with his feelings, how cruel. But she had been hurting so deeply that it had felt good in the moment to see his pain.

"And she would know." Hannah took a sip of wine before continuing, "It took Ryan ten years to finally hook Samantha."

"Yes, but we were lucky." Samantha placed the mug down and then looked directly at Angel. "Some people never have the opportunity for a second chance."

Angel's gaze fell to Hannah's baby, Maxine. Hadn't Angel seen her pregnancy as a second chance with Billy? And even as that hope died, she still dreamed of him walking through the door of O'Malley's in an Officer and Gentleman type of fashion. In way he had, minus the whole carrying her out in his arms thing. Life wasn't like the movies. She remembered Hoss' warning, 'Don't believe in fairy tales'.

"Do you want to hold her?"

Angel nodded. Had Hannah noticed the longing in Angel's eyes? When Hannah slid the warm bundle into Angel's arms she snuggled, cheek to cheek, inhaling the comforting scent babies naturally exuded. Angel had been so scared the first year of Gabby's life she barely enjoyed a moment of it. Believing she'd be a single parent all her life, she never thought of having another baby. Gabby deserved all her mom's love to replace an absent father. Holding Maxine stirred up Angel's hormones. Maybe in a couple of years she'd ask Billy to be a sperm donor so Gabby could have a sibling. Maybe she'd even ask him to donate the old fashion way. Then a hope so small it only had a chance to flicker as a fleeting thought, them as a real family. Perhaps, this was their second chance. Was she going to squander it away because she was afraid?

Gabby pirouetted back into the room. Upon noticing that her mom was now holding the baby, she stopped playing ballerina and ran over. "My turn," she ordered.

Angel shook her head. "She's not a toy."

"If it's okay with you, I'll put Maxine on a pillow and help Gabby hold her."

"Pleazeeeeeeeeeee, Mommy."

"Ok, but you have to sit still. And not the sit in church still and then you fidget like a monkey."

"I'll be as still as a church mouse."

Babies are cute, but five-year-olds are cuter. Then again Angel thought that about every stage of Gabby's life. Still, she wished she could keep Gabby five forever. No matter, she'd always be her little girl, always be that girl full of life and wonder. Perhaps Samantha was right. Had Angel really changed from that sixteen-year-old girl who fell so hopelessly in love with Billy? Her heart answered, no you haven't.

Thrilled with the chance to hold the baby, Gabby buzzed with excitement. As promised when Hannah placed the pillow with Maxine on Gabby's lap she sat rooted to her spot on the couch. That didn't stop the talking of course, but Gabby's sing song voice seemed to soothe the baby.

At that moment she heard the door open and close. Billy strode in. "Where's my girl—what the hell?"

Before Angel could say anything Samantha came to the rescue. "Hannah and I thought we'd welcome Angel and Gabby to the family."

Heat bloomed on Angel's cheeks. Would Billy think she'd given them the wrong impression? Being tongue-tied seemed to be a perpetual state when she was with Billy, except for when she was bitching at him.

"Look Daddy, I'm holding a baby." Gabby smiled proudly.

Angel frowned, disturbed by Gabby seeking Billy's approval. How many times over the years had Angel tried to win O'Malley's affections? She'd move heaven and hell before she'd let her little girl be disappointed like that.

"You're such a big girl," said Billy.

Gabby beamed with pride. How did he know the exact right thing to say? Angel really needed a chill pill or another glass of wine. *We bring our past hurts.* Samantha's words echoed in Angel's mind. Billy wasn't O'Malley. The sooner she got that through her thick skull the better off they'd all be.

"Daddy, when can I have a baby sister?"

Chapter 11

As soon as I can get your mom in my bed, he thought. His gaze landed on Angel, who stared back with wide eyes and cheeks tinged pink. *What was she thinking?*

If she could read his mind it'd probably scare her away. Billy wondered how she'd looked at three months, six months, and then at nine months pregnant. He imagined what it would have been like to put his hand on her belly and feel Gabby's tiny feet kicking beneath it. Thanks to O'Malley that chance had been stolen from him.

Honestly, Billy didn't know how he would've reacted to being a father at the age of eighteen. But the thought of Angel growing large awakened a fierce possessiveness in him now. This was their second chance to be a family. He didn't intend to walk out of her life again, no matter how much she tried to push him away.

"Well, honey, by the look of things, I don't think you're going to have to wait long," said Hannah.

Score one for Billy. Not only did he have his daughter on his team but with Hannah and Samantha rooting for him then he was that much closer to winning Angel's heart.

And to think when he first walked into the room he was in a state of panic thinking the two women had tried to warn Angel off.

"Well, we better leave you two lovebirds alone." Hannah gently picked up Maxine from the pillow.

"We're not...not—"

"Yet," said Hannah and Samantha simultaneously.

"Alone." Angel interrupted as she cut her eyes toward Gabby. "I was going to remind you we're not alone."

"So you ARE lovebirds?" Hannah grinned.

"That's not what I meant." Angel sputtered as she received a hug goodbye from each of the women.

"Quit while you're ahead," advised Billy. "Trust me, there's no winning with these two. You and I know what's going on. That's all that is important."

But once he was out of earshot at the door with his teammate's wives he whispered his thanks. "I appreciate the support ladies." Billy shot a glance over his shoulder to confirm he wasn't being overheard. "I'm trying not to scare Angel off."

Samantha turned and jabbed a finger onto his chest. "Don't fuck this up."

"Whoa, you've been hanging with the boys too much," responded Billy. She might have left reporting from the locker room behind, but she could still swear with the best of them.

"I only use the word for shock value. It's the only way to get you men to listen."

"I'm listening, I'm listening."

Hannah situated the baby into a contraption that looked like a backpack with a place for the baby's head, arms and legs to stick out. It reminded Billy of a turtle.

"You're a lucky man, Billy."

"I know." He imagined Angel holding Gabby at the same age as Maxine. He wondered if Angel packed the wall of photos or maybe there was a box of pictures he hadn't seen. "Thanks for welcoming them both," he repeated. Their doubtful looks made him add, "For real."

"Now go make a playmate for Gabby," said Hannah.

"I'm on it."

When he closed the door and turned to face Angel they traded heated glances. He looked away first and took a note of the time on the clock. Four long hours until Gabby's bedtime stretched out before him.

Deciding to make good use of the time he found reasons to touch her. His hand at the small of her back produced a startled gasp from her mouth. His fingertips generated goose bumps along her arm. She shivered as he breathed in her scent asking in a whisper what smelled so good. Each response from her amped him to the very edge of his control. At dinner she paid him back, torturing him by licking a knife with a seductive smile on her lips, while Gabby wasn't looking. His cock throbbed to be unleashed. Any moment he'd need a straightjacket to keep him from Angel's body.

But his ardor cooled as they watched Cinderella together. Like the family he pictured them being. After the movie ended he entered Gabby's bedroom as Angel grabbed a book. Spotting Billy, Gabby crossed her arms and said in a huffy voice. "No! I want Daddy to tell me a story."

Billy gently pulled the sheet over his daughter and tried not to smile at her pouty face. "I don't know any stories." He sat down next to her as Angel stretched out on the other side of the bed.

"Tell me how you and Mommy met."

Angel fussed with the sheet. "Oh, it was a long time ago. Daddy doesn't remember."

"Like it was yesterday," he said. Over the head of his daughter he gazed into Angel's shocked green eyes. "Let's see now. I lived eight hours away but that summer I attended the football camp right outside of your town. The heat wave that hit that summer was one for the record books. One humid night me and some of the guys decided to take a swim to cool off so we headed to the lake." He left out the part about sneaking out of the cabin. "A full moon shone on the lake and I saw a beautiful creature gliding through the water. I thought, could it be a mermaid?"

"That's silly. Everyone knows mermaids live in the ocean."

Billy's heart warmed, glad his daughter believed in mermaids. "True, but I thought she might be lost." Perhaps it was a trick of the light but the green eyes he stared into as he told the story looked misty and a little sad. Maybe, she'd been a lost soul. Maybe that's why they connected the way they did. Both were motherless teens, one with a father who didn't care and one with a father who cared to the point of suffocation. "As she swam away from us, I decided to catch the mermaid to prove she was real." He paused, reliving the moment in Angel's gaze.

"Then what happened?" asked Gabby.

"The mermaid was fast but I was faster. I caught the creature, kissed her, and then the water churned and bubbled as her tail turned into legs." He left out the fact that they were both skinny-dipping. "I asked the beauty on a date, and she told me to meet her at the town fair the following night."

"Where you won Ellie for her." Gabby hugged the pink elephant tightly to her chest.

So Gabby did know. Angel's dreamy smile told him she was reliving it in her mind.

Gabby yawned. "Did you love Mommy?"

"Yes," he said simply without adding that he never stopped loving her.

"Then why didn't you come back?"

"Gabby, it's time to go to sleep," whispered Angel.

Thinking Angel had left for Vegas he had no reason to come back. "I thought the mermaid swam back to the sea."

"But Mommy is a human."

Angel mesmerized him like no other girl had in the past or since. Did she cast a spell on him that night? "Hmmm, I don't know." No girl back home would swim naked in a lake like she belonged there, that was for sure.

"That means I'm a mermaid too! Like Ariel!"

"Billy, you've wound her all up. Bedtime stories are supposed to lull her to sleep." Angel stroked Gabby's forehead, which produced another wide yawn.

But she didn't sound mad, in fact she smiled at him. Not just any smile but one that made him think he was dreaming with his eyes wide opened. Or perhaps simply hallucinating.

He realized his mistake so long ago. Inexperienced, he took instead of gave. No wonder he hadn't satisfied her. Since then, he learned the sex playbook from cover to cover and he had a hell of a lot of practice.

Angel held his stare as Gabby fell asleep. After they quietly exited the room, Angel turned to him, mischief lit up her green eyes. "You know I let you catch me that night."

"I know." Billy didn't waste any time. Swooping his head down, he captured her lips with his. Instead of finesse he released his pent up passion to overwhelm her, stealing her breath before she could utter another protest. But she wasn't protesting. Changing the kiss to a slow and seductive one, it took every ounce of his will not to plunder and take. Her room, just steps away, beckoned but he wanted her in his bed where she belonged. Besides he planned to make her scream. Loud.

Chapter 12

Billy's kiss ignited the embers in Angel's heart into a flame that roared through her blood until her body burned from within. His hands ran down along her curves then back up, one finding its way beneath her shirt, closing around her breast. The other wound its way through her hair. Responding with a moan, she pressed against him.

"Tell me you don't want this. Tell me now if you don't, because your body is talking to me in a whole other language," he said, his voice husky with need.

She couldn't even claim that her body was betraying her. Mind, body, and soul all demanded a release only Billy could provide. Her heart wanted more. It yearned for something greater. But for now she would take what she could get. "I do. I mean, I do. Want this," she said, stumbling over the words.

He smiled as he picked her up then carried her like a groom on their wedding night. When he stepped over the threshold of his room, sadness caromed inside her heart. All those wasted years. Could they recapture the pureness of the love they once shared?

He placed her on his unmade king-sized bed. With her attention focused on Billy stripping off his shirt and pants, she couldn't say what his room looked like. But his ripped abs she could describe in great detail. The skin stretched across his muscles so tightly she feared her nails might tear it. So when she reached out, she did so gently, using the pads of her fingers to trail a path along the labyrinth of ridges. His skin warmed under her light touch and she could feel the raw power rippling beneath. The fabric on his form fitting boxer briefs tented impressively with proof of his arousal. She attempted to delve down lower, but he gripped her hand tightly.

"Patience," he said in a teasing tone.

Patience? She didn't know how to be with this older, more controlled version of Billy. They'd always been so eager, so desperate to be together.

Stretching out over her, he kissed her long and deep. Old feelings resurfaced whirling with new complex emotions that she didn't understand. Was he kissing the girl she once was or the woman she was now? Did he even see a difference? Was there a difference?

His lips left hers to take off her shirt and bra. Goosebumps skittered along her skin as he placed tender kisses along her collarbone. His mouth closed over her breast, she bucked beneath him. Billy growled his approval. Hands she remembered as unsure now masterfully played along her body. He continued down and she self-consciously tried to cover the silvery lines marring her skin, but he brushed her hands away.

"You are beautiful, Angel. All of you." He licked the lines proving his words. "I wish I was there for you." Then he gently kissed her stomach before trailing more kisses downward.

She stilled when he reached the apex of her thighs and breathed in her scent. That was new. He took a taste and she stopped comparing notes of the past and present.

"Ah, Angel. I didn't know what I was doing back then."

He stroked his thumb up along her clit and she nearly jumped out of her skin. "Neither of us did," she squeaked. God, she still didn't.

"You always knew how to make me crazy with want." He gazed into her eyes before looking down at her pussy and said, "I swear I'm about to make it up to you."

The pace of his tongue was tortuously slow. She relaxed, opening up to him, urging for more. Was this some sort of Kama Sutra thing? If so she didn't like it and she cried out in frustration. He laughed against her and the vibration of his mouth nearly made her come. In slight increments he increased the pressure of his tongue until she was grabbing fistful of sheets and gulping for air. Only then did he step up the speed.

Two of his fingers slid inside, but as magical as they were, were not enough, she needed all of him. Every. Last. Inch.

She needed his body on top of hers. In her. To feel that connection between them again.

Every fiber of her being pooled to her pussy and she came in a glorious release as she shouted his name into the silent room. Minutes later she opened her eyes to find him memorizing her face as if he expected her to disappear at any moment. The only way she'd be motivated to move is if Gabby had awakened from the shouts of her mother.

Angel's mommy senses perked up and she listened for a disturbance in the night.

"She's still asleep," Billy whispered.

She almost laughed. They used to have to worry about her father bursting into her room and now they skipped right to the worrying about their daughter ruining the moment. "Then let's finish up before she wakes."

"Finish?" Billy arched an eyebrow. "Angel, we're just getting started."

She smiled at the implications but tried to scoot away from him and reached for the nightstand drawer.

"Where do you think you're going?" he asked, amusement in his voice.

"Getting a condom." Gabby could ask for a baby sister, but that wasn't going to happen any time soon.

"I don't keep them there." Billy got up and walked to his dresser, opening the top drawer. Striding back he tossed three condoms onto the bed. Now it was her turn to arch an eyebrow.

"Like I said, we're just getting started."

Moving to her knees she grabbed one of the foil packets as he peeled off his boxer briefs. Dear God, did *that* get bigger too? Maybe, it had just been too long since she'd seen one.

"Stop staring at it like it's got three heads."

Angel's grin turned saucy. "Kinky."

He pushed her onto her back. "You won't need kink after I'm done with you." He spread her legs wide. He entered her slowly and her eyes fluttered shut in the sweet relief of it.

"Open your eyes," he demanded.

She did as she was told. In his gaze she recognized her Billy. The one who wrote her a poem, the one who saw beyond the tough girl façade, the one who was her first and only one.

"There you are, Angel," he whispered, brushing away a strand of her hair. "I missed you."

"Oh, Billy, I…" *I love you.* "…I missed you too." She tightened around him in a bid for him to move. He complied, his body, a mass of strewn muscle, moved with the sleek grace of a panther.

Could thrusts be tender? His were. Each one hit something deep inside her, something more powerful than the physical. Her body hummed with bliss. Her hands explored his back before settling on his butt. Angel could feel the strength he held in check behind each stroke. She thought she might die if he didn't go faster, she might die if he did. Digging her nails into his flesh, she urged him to go faster as the pressure surged to a breaking point. Angel reached the highest of high then went into a freefall of intense pleasure.

She came apart in his arms and she knew she'd never be whole again. Knew she wanted the fairy tale even if it meant risking a tragic Shakespearean end.

Chapter 13

How had he lived without her? How had he breathed?

Desperate gasps of pleasure escaped her mouth. Her need fueled his, but he was determined to give and not to take. She tightened around him and he knew she was close. Lifting her hips, he held them in place as he drove in harder, deeper, barely able to hold on to the edge of control. The cry of her release echoed in the room signaled his victory. The rush of her liquid heat surrounded his cock as he pumped in and out, riding out her orgasm with his own.

Unable to hold himself up, Billy rolled off before he crushed her under his full weight. There was no way she wasn't sexually satisfied. "There's no faking that," he said without thinking.

"Is that what this was about?"

Before she could scoot off the bed Billy grabbed her wrist. This time he used his power not to seduce but to control. He pulled her back underneath him. His cock responded with interest, but he ignored it. He wanted answers, and he was going to get them. Something wasn't right about the way things ended, but he couldn't put his finger on it. "Can you blame me? That's why you broke up with me."

"That's not the reason," she said as she struggled to get away.

Stunned by her answer, he almost let her, but then he pressed his weight against her body. "Then why?"

"It was so long ago." Defeated, her body fell limp beneath him. "Does it matter?"

"It damn well matters," he admitted. In the cocoon of his room, lying skin to skin, he risked his soul by being raw and balls to the walls honest. He hoped Angel would be too. "You broke my heart. I deserve to know why."

Tear sprung in Angel's eyes. "I thought you'd be better off without me."

More confused than ever he asked, "What?"

"O'Malley told me you'd gotten into a fight with your father over me and you threatened to drop out of school. He said if I really loved you, I'd let you go."

Holy Hell. How had O'Malley known about the argument? Billy's coach had caught him breaking curfew to meet up with Angel and the infraction was reported to his father who then must have conspired with Angel's father to end it. It made perfect sense. Why hadn't Billy realized this before? But once O'Malley knew about Angel's pregnancy why had he kept it from Billy? Again his search for answers led only to more questions. A conversation with his father was long overdue.

"Say something."

He looked back into Angel's pleading eyes. "Ah Angel, how could I be better off without my heart."

Her tears spilled over. "Billy, I'm so sorry."

"For what Angel? For loving me?"

Angel placed her hand on his cheek. "I did, Billy."

He rolled off of her for a second time. Drawing up his legs, he rested his forearms on his knees and clasped his hands. "But not any more?"

Angel sat up beside him, pulling the sheet around her. "We were kids. Hell, in a lot of ways we still are."

He agreed with the first part of her statement but not the second. Billy just made love to her with all the feelings of a man in love. At age twenty-two Angel was more woman than he could probably handle. She raised a child on her own while earning a nursing degree and coddling a gambling addicted father. The woman deserved a break. And Gabby deserved a family. "What we had together was real. We owe it to ourselves to give it a shot."

"What if it doesn't work out?"

"What if it does?" he countered.

"But what if it doesn't?" she repeated. "It's not fair for Gabby to get her hopes up."

She had a point. He'd hate to see Gabby upset, never mind be the cause of it. Still, if there was any chance they could give their daughter a normal family life, then they should take it. "It would be more unfair to Gabby if we didn't try."

The bathroom light cast a surreal glow onto the bed as if marking the moment as one happening in an alternate universe. Because no one would believe that Billy Burner, the womanizing pro football player, was not only begging for a second chance, but using his child as leverage. Justifying this means to an end was simple; it wasn't what was best for him, but what was best for them as a family.

He waited in the blessed silence. At least he wasn't hearing a 'no' from those swollen kissed lips.

"Okay—"

He moved to kiss her, but she placed a firm hand on his chest.

"But there are rules," she continued.

He brushed his thumb along her cheekbone. "I remember a girl who didn't like rules."

"Well, I'm a mom now."

"I'm not a child who needs rules."

"No, but we have one together. And these rules are for Gabby's sake."

Billy fell back to the mattress with a thud. "Okay, shoot."

"Number one. No outward displays of affection. No 'kissing' mommy goodbye."

"I'll try to restrain myself," he said, his voice laced in sarcasm.

"Number two. No other women."

He supposed his ladies' man reputation would give any woman pause, but he never cheated on a woman. Of course that was because since Angel he'd never been in a steady relationship. Still, he decided to have some fun with her and asked, "And that rule is for Gabby?"

She turned from her sitting position to look at him. "Well, no, not exactly."

Billy smiled, but then he grew serious. "That's a two way street. What goes for me goes for you. No other men."

"I haven't even been on the road until tonight." She rolled her eyes. "Rule three."

If she said no sex Billy swore he'd argue the point by making love to her again until she begged for release. And what did she mean by 'she hadn't been on the road'? Had she never had sex after him? Impossible.

"I go back to my bed each night."

Okay so it wasn't a 'no sex' clause, but damn it, they were adults. The days of sneaking around were long over. He wanted to wake up with Angel in his arms. To pull her close as dawn broke. To feel her warm body next to his, to hear her breathe while she slept, and to wake her up in the most pleasant of ways. "No."

"Gabby is not stupid. If she sees us sharing a bedroom, she'll start asking questions."

"But."

"Those are my terms."

Billy blew out a breath. He reminded himself of his game plan. What was his game plan again? Oh yeah, patience. So far his strategy was working like a charm. He already made love to her; now he had to prove to her that they belonged together. Always had.

"Agreed." He added a silent rule of his own, to make love to her each night until she was too weak to get out of his bed, never mind walk back to her room. With that in mind he pulled Angel on top of him and kissed her. The taste of her lips filled him with hunger. The feel of her naked skin ignited his blood. Her scent of vanilla intoxicated him. Rolling to the side, limbs entwined until the heat they generated seem to meld them together as one. He breathed her in as if it was the last breath he'd ever take. If she ever left him again, he felt sure that it would be.

Chapter 14

For once Angel felt like she fit in. Shocking, considering she currently lounged in the plush seating area of the owner's skybox at the stadium with Samantha and Hannah.

Behind them stood a mahogany bar with top end liquor, a poker table and a couple of high tables with stools. Off to the side stood a large chalkboard on an easel and on the other a lit up trophy case stood as a testament to the team's success. Television screens hung about the room so none of the action would be missed. A group of high-powered men talked football and business deals. Hell, minutes ago she was introduced to the Governor.

Samantha had her eyes on the game, but Angel could tell she was listening with a reporter's ear. Though the other wives and girlfriends sat in the seating just outside the box, a wall of glass separated them. At first Angel received some dirty looks from the other women, but Hannah said not to worry. The owner loved the good publicity he received from having a supermodel and a probable future Pulitzer Prize winner grace his skybox. And now Angel served in the same role. After a photo of her coming out of

Billy's apartment building ended up plastered all over the New York gossip pages, she received an invite from the owner's wife. Instead of the scandal she'd feared they'd report, the press treated the story as a star-crossed lovers tale. She guessed they were in a good mood that day.

Concerned about the invite, Angel was grateful Hannah had taken her under her wing. When Angel fell in love with a sleek pair of faux leather pants, she put it back on the rack thinking that such clothes would be more appropriate for a pool hall. Then Hannah took it off the rack suggesting a smart looking black and white glen plaid jacket along with a crisp white blouse that flowed loosely about Angel's hips. The outfit cost more than Angel would spend in an entire year for clothes but Billy had slipped her his credit card before she'd left and said 'have fun'. Angel blushed when Hannah tossed in several silky bras and matching panties saying Billy deserved something too.

"Oh, no."

Angel followed Samantha's gaze. The owner's daughter arrived with a flourish of laughter. Hayden Middleton was a tabloid reporter's wet dream. The curvy heiress to a fortune was as morally bankrupt as she was rich. As she paused at the top of the stairs the fake smile turned into a mean girl smirk that marred her otherwise pretty features. "So who's this? Don't tell me. Burner's baby mama?"

Turning her back, Angel clenched her jaw in an effort not to respond to the cutting barb. For Gabby's future, and for Billy's, she decided to remain silent despite the comment's sting. So much for thinking she fit in.

Not to be ignored, Hayden stepped down, and with a perfectly manicured hand snagged a cone of candied nuts.

She leaned against the glass, away from the game in progress. "What's your brat anyway? Boy? Girl?"

Angel's eyes narrowed in anger.

"What, no answer?" Hayden popped a nut into her mouth. "Surprised Burner doesn't have a litter. Of course, who knows? Maybe he does."

Angel's right hand curled into a fist. If this were O'Malley's, Angel would've broken a cue stick over the bitch's head. It was one thing to disparage Angel's reputation but Gabby's? Oh hell no. She went to lunge at Hayden but Samantha placed a firm grip over Angel's hand.

"Why, Hayden, how lovely to see you," Hannah twirled a piece of her long blonde hair around her finger. "And here I thought you'd still be on your court-ordered vacation."

"You're going to pay for that."

"Going to run to daddy?" Samantha chimed in.

In true brat style, Hayden stomped back up the few steps and joined the group of men. Angel released a slow breath and Samantha let go of her hand.

"Thank you," Angel said. Realizing they saved her from making a scene, she added, "I hope I'm not going to get you into trouble."

"Don't mind her. 'Hoyden' is just pissed because I refuse to sign on for her new reality show," said Hannah.

Grinning, Samantha relaxed back into her seat. "Besides I'm pretty sure we just saved Hayden's life."

Angel vowed Gabby wouldn't end up like Hayden, princess room be damned. Her daughter would learn the value of a dollar and work for what she wanted. Angel needed to lay down the law with Billy. She was adding some new rules. No more arriving home after every practice with a new toy for Gabby. No more sneaking her a cookie after every meal.

Angel bit her lip each time, understanding he was trying to make up for lost time. Still, Billy had to start thinking of what was best for their daughter's future. With money tight Angel had scrimped for healthy foods and left the desserts for special occasions. Gabby still had no idea what soda even tasted like. God help them all if she ever did. Billy had yet to hear a whine out of Gabby. He was in for a rude awakening.

"No, not him," groaned Hayden. "There goes the season."

A sudden hush fell over the room and Angel turned her attention back to the field where a Cougar player lay prone on the turf. With his helmet on she couldn't tell who it was. She desperately searched for Billy, not taking a breath until she spotted him. Standing in profile, his long blond locks flowed from beneath his helmet. His hair identified him even before she noticed the number and name on his jersey.

A quick glance at her friend's faces told Angel it wasn't one of their husbands either.

"Our quarterback." Samantha winced at the TV close-up. "Look at his leg. His career is probably over."

Angel stared up at the large monitor and watched the replay in horror. That could have been Billy.

Chapter 15

Billy knew from the sound of muzzled gunfire that Todd had just broken his leg.

Baker, the defensive end from the Warriors, leapt up from the pile signaling frantically to the sideline and screaming, "Get somebody out here, get somebody out here now."

Writhing, Todd grabbed both sides of his helmet then pounded the turf with his fists. Suddenly he went still, so still that Billy prayed it was just shock kicking in. He eyed the bone protruding from Todd's bloody sock.

"Out of the way." The medical team from both sides rushed over to the gruesome scene.

The offensive coordinator shouted for Billy, Miller and the backup quarterback, Liam McQueen to get over to the bench to review some plays. The Cougars liked to run a two tight end formation but since Terell never practiced with the second string, Billy would be the McQueen's main target. If the coach let him throw that is.

Not that the former first round draft pick didn't have skills, but he squandered them away letting the fame go to his head, skipping practice like he was too good for it and boozing it up to the point of being forced into rehab.

Once his career tanked and hit rock bottom, he found God. Funny how that happens. Clean and sober McQueen rededicated himself to football, but none of the teams were buying it except for the Cougars. He didn't know if the owner did it for the publicity or because he believed in second chances like he said during the off-season press conference announcing the signing.

For Billy it amounted to one big distraction. Billy knew he had to put that all aside. It was important for him to believe in McQueen, now the leader of the offense. Billy did his best to concentrate on the plays, but an injury like the one Todd sustained could rattle even the toughest of players. Ten minutes went by and the medical team was still working on him.

Once McQueen started throwing warm-up passes along the sidelines, Billy ran back out. A pressure cast surrounded Todd's leg. Billy and a couple of the guys lifted him onto the stretcher, then to the golf cart.

"I'll be back," Todd said.

"Sure you will." But from the lack of jibes and ribs, everyone knew there would be no comebacks for their teammate.

A roar of cheers rose up for the injured quarterback as he exited the stadium on the back of the cart. Then just as quickly, a flurry of boos rang down as his replacement ran onto the field. McQueen joined the huddle like he didn't hear a thing.

"Hope you're feeling the Holy Spirit," Miller joked.

"Let's get one thing straight. God doesn't care who wins this football game," said McQueen. After a few nods of respect he added, "Burner break at the 10, cut back to the 20, the ball will be there."

"Coach called for the run." As a running back, Miller wanted the ball.

"The D, hell, everyone in this stadium, is expecting that."

McQueen was looking to make a statement with a thirty-yard pass, but Billy didn't argue; there wasn't time. The game clock ticked down.

On the snap Billy broke down the field. The defender matched him step for step, but Billy stopped on a dime at the ten and hit the twenty-yard line just as the ball arrived. Just like in practice. But he wasn't done yet. The defender who tried to scramble back fell at his feet as Billy performed his signature move, the Turn and Burn, and jumped over the prone body of the defender and ran the ball into the end zone.

The crowd erupted.

A couple of teammates joined him in the celebration. He looked back to see McQueen on his knees with his hands in the air as if he were being anointed by the angels. What happened to 'God doesn't care who wins this football game'?

Speaking of which, he wondered if his Angel witnessed the spectacular touchdown.

In the locker room Billy watched as frenzied reporters surrounded McQueen. They'd already dubbed the new quarterback's celebration move the McQuing. McQueen shrugged off the attention, nodding at Billy with a grace so unlike his old ways.

A few reporters made their way to Billy's locker. After countless times of sticking his own foot in his mouth, Billy kept to his stock answers.

As he left the locker room the adrenaline from the win started to wear off. The bumps and bruises settled in his body. All he wanted right now was his whirlpool tub and an ice-cold beer.

And Angel.

He spotted her easily among the crowd in the greeting room. Despite her average height, she stood out to him. Hot damn, those leather pants hugged her ass. Angel upped her game by wearing pin-up red lipstick instead of her signature purple. His cock approved. Great, the one body part that hadn't ached now caused him the most discomfort. He hoped they could sneak in a quickie before picking up Gabby from the neighbors.

Catcalls were directed towards her and he wasted no time marking his territory. Planting a big kiss on her lips, he made it clear to his teammates that Angel belonged to him.

Chapter 16

Billy kissed her in front of everyone. A kiss? It was more like a claiming. What else would you call it when a man pulls you into his arms and lifts you a foot off the ground in a bruising kiss?

Not that she was complaining. Billy could kiss her anywhere, at anytime, and anyway he wanted to. Except in front of Gabby. Perhaps it was time to lift that rule. She hated putting him on the spot when Gabby expected him to kiss Mommy.

Unable to clear her head, Angel clung to him for a few moments after he ended the kiss. Billy introduced her to Ryan Terell, Samantha's husband; Jake Miller, Hannah's husband; and Liam McQueen, the playboy turned Born Again Christian. She remembered watching him play years ago. You didn't work in a pub and not see your share of football games.

Hannah and Samantha joined the group. "Jake, I had a little run in with Hayden."

"Ah, Hannah."

"It was my fault," Angel defended her friend.

"No, it was Hayden's fault." Samantha directed her gaze at Billy. "She called Angel your baby mama, then implied Gabby was part of a litter."

"What!" The muscles in Billy's jaw clenched like a wolf ready to tear into its prey.

"So before Angel could release that fist of hers, I jumped in to deflect Hayden's wrath to me," Hannah explained.

Angel received a proud look from Billy. "Next time punch her."

"What she needs is a good spanking," piped in McQueen.

Angel thought she saw a gleam in Hannah's eye and knew the quarterback was in trouble.

"Liam, you're just the man to give her one."

"Stop matchmaking, woman," said her husband.

Samantha, ever the journalist, said, "It would be epic, I can see it now," She placed her hand in the air like it was a headline. "Sinner and saint go head to head."

"Hah," Liam laughed. "Sure, throw the Christian into the lioness' den."

Miller smacked Liam on his non-throwing arms shoulder. "Come on, take one for the team."

"On the field, I'm your man. Off it, I'm my own man." Liam said goodbye and headed out ahead of the group.

Billy nodded to the exit and Angel followed his lead.

"Hey Burner, five Gs? I'll even spot you 3 points?" offered Jake.

"Should never bet with your heart, my friend," said Billy.

Angel's heart dropped into her stomach. *A bet?*

As they came out of the players exit, three groupies surrounded Billy even though he was holding her hand. Before they could jostle her away, he pulled her closer.

"Billy, pick me," one pleaded.

"Sorry ladies, I'm taken."

Angel barely registered his words or the sour looks thrown her way from the other women. How many times had she argued with her father over his gambling addiction? How many times had she had to hustle a pool game because her father literally gambled the milk money away?

In the car, Billy tried to engage her in conversation but she kept looking out the window to avoid a confrontation. Not now. She wanted one more night in his arms. One more night before the fairy tale ended with a not so happily ever after.

"Are you mad about those women?"

She wasn't mad. She wasn't exactly thrilled about it either, but really did trust Billy when it came to other women.

"It's going to happen, even when word gets around that I have a girlfriend. Hell, it still happens to the married players."

"I'm not upset about that."

Billy blew out a breath. "Can you give me a clue then to what you are upset about?"

She remained silent, unable to express the feelings of disappointment.

"Is it the run in with Hayden?"

"It's about your gambling," she blurted.

"Gambling? What the fuck? Wait, you mean that bet I made with Jake?"

She nodded. Looking out the window again, she waited for the explanations. That's how it starts. Then the denials and soon after that, the outright lies.

"It's a friendly bet, Angel. Our college teams are playing against each other this weekend, it's not gambling."

She let her silence answer for her.

"Jesus, Angel you hustled pool."

He might as well have taken a cue stick and stabbed her in the heart. She hustled pool for food money, not for the thrill of it, at least not since she became a mom. "It's not the same thing. Pool is a game of skill," she argued.

A game of angles and patterns Angel could read a table like a pool shark savant. More importantly, she picked out her marks with the same uncanny ability. Through teary eyes she focused on Billy's tight grip on the steering wheel.

"I'm not your father Angel. I'm not an addict."

And there it was. Her heart clenched in agony. How many times had her father uttered those words? Perhaps she was wrong putting Billy in the same category as O'Malley, but Angel had been through it before and she wouldn't let history repeat itself. Not for her, and certainly not for Gabby.

Chapter 17

That Saturday Billy tried to focus on the college football game on his state of the art screen. Miller and Terell joined him while Angel went out to lunch with their wives. He hoped Hannah and Samantha could talk some sense into Angel. She wasn't jealous over the groupies, or mad about being dissed by Hayden, no, it was all about the stupid bet.

He had five Gs riding on this game, but it wasn't about the money. Normally, he'd be ribbing Miller about his team's dismal play, but Angel had Billy turned inside out. She wouldn't listen to reason. In front of Gabby, she was almost herself, but each night Angel refused to come to his room.

Worse, she started letting him tuck in Gabby by himself like she was preparing him for shared custody. *Fuck that.* The three of them were a family. And families worked shit out. Tonight he'd promise her anything. And if that didn't work, he'd throw her over his shoulder and toss her onto his bed then make love to her until she felt like they were a part of each other.

"Heard you're in the dog house." Miller said.

Billy shrugged. "She over reacted," he said without conviction.

"Can't say that I blame her. Sammy said her father lost everything."

"I know. I know. But I'm nothing like her father."

"We can call off the bet." Miller's mischievous grin gave him away.

Billy laughed. "Sure, cause your team is losing."

The grin grew wider. "Just trying to help."

"I have an idea," said Terell. "Why not donate the winnings to charity."

"That sounds like Samantha's idea."

"Shut up, Miller." Terell flicked a pretzel at him.

Gabby skipped into the room wearing a pink dress and her rhinestone tiara. She curtsied liked she was receiving royalty instead of three large football players. Though facing a five-year-old girl seemed to turn such men into knights instead of brutes. She scooted onto Billy's lap. Pointing to the screen she asked, "Daddy, why are those men hugging?

Miller and Terell laughed, and Billy smiled. "It's called a huddle." Before he could explain further she spoke again.

"Do you want to hear a joke?" Gabby asked.

"Of course, we do," Miller responded.

"Knock, knock."

"Who's there?" Terell asked.

"Gabriela." She played with the frilly hem of her dress.

"Gabriela who?" This time it was Miller.

"Gabriela O'Malley Burner," she said in a rush. She broke into a fit of giggles like it was the funniest joke in the universe.

The three men joined in with raucous laughter. But it wasn't lost on Billy that she added his last name. He gave her a kiss on the cheek. As he got up, he shifted her from his lap to his hip. "I have a cookie with your name on it."

Angel didn't have to know. The special occasion dessert rule was ridiculous. Anyway, watching a football game was a special occasion. What damage could the occasional cookie or two do?

Once in the kitchen he handed a cookie to Gabby, but instead of gobbling it up, she tilted her head and examined both sides. "Where's my name?"

Did all five-year olds take things so literally? Gabriela O'Malley Burner. He wanted it to be legal. Realizing he hadn't uttered the words yet, though he felt them with all his heart, he said, "I love you, Gabby."

"I love you too, Daddy." She planted a kiss on his cheek before taking a big bite of the cookie.

I love you, you love me. Just like that. So easy. So simple. So why hadn't he said it to Angel yet? He certainly showed his love. In many ways, in and out of the bedroom.

"Touchdown!" Jake's shout from the living room echoed through the apartment.

The bet. He showed his love, except, for when it counted. Except, for when it mattered most.

So what if she was being unreasonable? So what if he looked like a pussy for backing out of the bet? He denied her the one thing she needed to feel safe. All the money he had couldn't do that. Only Billy could.

Tonight, he'd tell Angel he was sorry and mean it. Tell her he was in love with her. Tell her he wanted it be official.

Angel O'Malley Burner. His future wife. His forever love.

After his teammates left, Billy prepared dinner while Gabby played in her room with the elusive Lucy. The only evidence of the cat's existence was the occasional present on the carpet and Billy's own occasional sneezes.

Just as he put the roast in the oven, the doorman called. His father was downstairs. He should've known this was coming. After the story hit the papers of his 'long-lost' daughter he had called his father to break the news. He didn't take it well. "Send him up."

Fearing Gabby might overhear something she shouldn't, Billy met him outside the apartment in the hallway. "Why the sudden visit, Dad?"

Except for a bigger gut, his father looked like the same tank who'd come to blows with his seventeen-year-old son. By then Billy had already been taller. But now Billy had also packed on a professional athlete's muscle. His father no longer intimidated him.

"I came to talk some sense into you. Let's go inside. I could use a beer."

"We need to talk here." Billy peeked through the opening of the door to make sure Gabby hadn't left her room.

"Oh, I see. A model? Playmate?"

"Neither." Billy responded through clench teeth. "It's my daughter."

"I knew it." He raked his hand through a shorter version of his son's. "That O'Malley bitch is trying to squeeze money out of you just like her old man did me."

Billy blinked as the realization dawn. "You paid off O'Malley to get rid of Angel?" *Please God, don't let it be true.*

"The five grand was well worth it. I wasn't about to let you ruin your football career. O'Malley hit me up for another ten grand to put that tramp's brat up for adoption."

Billy's slammed his fist onto his father's jaw. When the bastard hit the wall and slid to the carpet, he didn't feel an ounce of remorse. "I knew you dreamed of having a son in the NFL, but that's no excuse for what you did.

"Blame O'Malley." Slowly regaining his feet, his dad swiped away a trickle of blood from his lips. "He was more than happy to settle his stack of markers."

If O'Malley were still alive Billy would have punched him in the jaw too. Leaving Angel and Gabby penniless and homeless was the least of O'Malley's gambling addiction fallout.

Suddenly Angel's reaction to Billy's bet didn't seem so unreasonable.

Chapter 18

As Angel waited for the elevator to glide upstairs, she stared at the business card Hannah had given her at lunch. O'Malley's didn't do therapy. That's what her father always said when she pleaded with him to get help for his gambling addiction.

But if someone like Hannah admitted to needing a therapist for what she called her 'mommy dearest' issues, then maybe Angel could get help too. When Billy made that bet she'd deflected all the fears and insecurities from years of O'Malley's addiction onto him. Billy had never lied or tried to manipulate her. He'd been nothing but kind, loving, and generous. She hoped he'd understand. Hoped he wouldn't call her crazy because she needed therapy. Hoped he'd forgive her.

The doors of the elevator slid open. She froze after taking two steps out into the hall. An older man with the same colored hair as Billy's looked at her with disgust. His father.

"Well look at you, all dolled up with my son's money."

"You will not speak to her that way." Billy's expression softened and he motioned Angel to come to him.

Angel sidestepped Mr. Burner and rushed into Billy's waiting arms. "Is Gabby okay?"

"Yes, she's playing in her room. I'm almost done here. Why don't you head inside too?'

Billy's father glared at her. "Not so fast. Admit that you knew about the money."

"What money?" Angel's heart pounded as if she climbed all forty-four stories.

"Dad!" Billy took her hands. His face a death mask of pain. "Angel, I don't know how to tell you than to just say it. My father paid off yours to get you to break up with me."

What? Angel almost laughed. Did she hear that right? By the way Billy's face tightened in distress, she knew he struggled with something else.

"There's more." His thumbs ran along her hands in a caress. "Did O'Malley try to talk you into adoption?"

"He had a social worker come to the hospital, but... oh my God! No, no, no." God, if she didn't need therapy before, she sure did now. How could two fathers be so cruel to their children, to their grandchild? "I refused. I couldn't, I just couldn't. She was a part of you, a part of us."

Billy pulled her into a tight embrace. "You're a strong woman, Angel." He hugged her even tighter. "Thank God."

"Don't be stupid, Billy. She got pregnant on purpose," Mr. Burner accused.

Before Angel could deny it, Billy defended her. "Don't put that at her feet. I'm the one who didn't wear a condom."

"You can dress her up Billy, but she'll always be a slut."

Billy placed Angel behind his back as he turned to meet his father head on. "She was never that. In fact, she's the one with a college degree. Not the son who you pushed and pushed to declare early for the NFL draft. Now go."

Tears spilled from her eyes. No one had ever stuck up for her like that.

Up against his back, she could feel the tenseness in his muscles and how hard he was trying to keep himself in check. His father didn't say a word as he pushed the down button.

Billy took a deep breath. "Dad, if you decide to be a part of my family, you'll have to apologize to Angel. And to your granddaughter." The doors opened. "Her name is Gabriela. Gabriela O'Malley Burner."

Without a word Billy's father stepped into the elevator.

As the doors slid closed, Angel squeezed his arm. "I'm so sorry, Billy." She knew how hard it was for Billy to stand up to his father. She realized that she and Gabby weren't the only ones hurt by O'Malley's obsessive gambling. Billy had missed the first five years of his daughter's life. But fate had given them a second chance and Angel almost threw it away.

"Let's go inside." Once in the living room Billy turned to her. "Angel, I," He tipped up her chin with his finger. "Aww, Baby, I'm sorry he made you cry."

"I'm not crying about that. These are happy tears."

"Happy tears?" Billy scratched his head. "I'm confused."

"You defended me. Believed in me."

"Always." He brushed her tears away. "Can you try to believe in me too? Believe that I will never, never place another bet in my life. Believe that I would never hurt you or Gabby." He got down on one knee and held both her hands. "Believe that I will always love you. Marry me, my Angel."

Looking down into his sincere blue eyes, her fears washed away on a wave of intense love. "I do believe in you." Fresh tears sprung in her eyes. "I love you, Billy. I never stopped."

A stomp of a foot sounded from the hallway. "Mommy, you're supposed to say yes!"

Billy and Angel broke into laughter. Releasing one of her hands, Billy held out an arm. "Come on, Gabby, huddle up."

Gabby ran over throwing her arms around her Daddy's neck. He stood and wrapped them both in a warm hug. "Mommy, huddle up means group hug in football."

Bounding out of Gabby's room even Lucy seemed to know. She weaved around Billy and Angel's ankles then rubbed her face against Billy's pant leg.

"Can I have a cookie?"

"No, honey, you had one earlier," he said with surprising firmness.

Angel hid her smile when she saw how equally surprised their daughter was. Gabby's bottom lip started to quiver. Oh boy, Billy was about to get a taste of a five-year-old's wrath. Angel slipped away from the hug.

"Wait! Where are you going?"

The panic in his voice brooked no sympathy from Angel. "To take a bath," she said. "With bubbles. And maybe a beer."

"But...but."

Gabby's wail filled the air.

"Welcome to fatherhood, Billy," she said as she sashayed down the hall. Smiling she whispered, "And welcome to your happily ever after, Angel."

Epilogue

H ayden hated weddings. Okay, maybe hate was too strong of a word. But the word fit perfectly for how she felt about her father's order to attend Billy Burner's nuptials as the Middleton family representative. Her father lectured constantly about the importance of treating the football team like family. Too bad he didn't extend the same courtesy to his own daughter.

Billy and Angel wasted no time after the engagement, planning a no-fuss wedding at the courthouse. That was until Hannah and Samantha took over, rescheduling the ceremony for the team's bye week.

The bride twirled, showing off the beautiful wedding dress designed by Hannah. Only the supermodel could pull off such a masterpiece in a month. The classic ball gown skirt swirled with the perfection of a storybook princess while the woven white leather rock star inspired bodice suited Angel's hard edge. Dressed in an eighteenth century styled suit, the groom wore his mane of blond hair in a slick ponytail that his daughter was currently tugging on.

Gabriela, who was the picture of cuteness, almost made Hayden feel maternal.

Almost. She looked away before the sickening sweet scene ruined her foul mood.

Hayden's gaze landed on Liam McQueen, the reformed bad boy quarterback of the Cougars. The press was currently hailing him the Savior of the Cougars' season. She was surprised Liam wasn't home having milk and cookies instead of nursing what looked like a Scotch. Hating his holier than thou attitude, she itched to mess with him. Could the choirboy be tempted to sin again? Challenge accepted. Just the something she needed to distract her from her latest run in with the paparazzi.

Oh, shit. Liam had just caught her staring. Staring? More like ogling. With a smile created for endorsements, the quarterback strolled over without breaking eye contact. She toyed with her necklace, those clear brown eyes reminding her of the chocolate diamonds draped around her neck.

"Hey Hayden." His six-foot-three frame now towered over her. The tux fit his wide shoulders to perfection.

The memory of the half-naked spread he did for Men's Health lit up her brain. And other places too. She stalled unable to come up with anything. She told herself it would be far too easy to seduce him. Not worth her time. Falling back into bitch mode where she felt most at home, she said in a withering tone, "It's hello, not hay. Where did you grow up, in a barn? Oh wait, you did."

"Lighten up. It's a wedding, not a funeral."

He smacked her rump. With only the gold silk of her dress between her ass and his hand, she gasped with shock and yes, a tiny zing of pleasure. Where had that come from? Shock won out and she glared at him. With a little push, he urged her out onto the dance floor. Did the caveman think she'd dance with him?

"Heads up," he said. "Incoming pass."

What was that supposed to mean? By the time she caught sight of the bridal bouquet it was already too late. The cluster of purple lilies sailed over a bevy of vying females and smacked Hayden on the head. Cameras flashed as the flowers landed at her feet and women scrambled for the prize.

Hayden kicked the bouquet. How many of the attendees caught that on video? Her father was going to kill her. She stalked over to Liam and poked him in the chest.

She ignored the drum of his heart beneath her finger, the way it pounded in sync with hers. Ignored the spark of electricity firing up her body as if her arm were some sort of lightening rod. "Don't ever touch me again."

Hayden stormed out the door, losing a shoe in the process, but she wasn't going back for it, even if she had once stroked the pair like a long lost lover.

She hated weddings. And she hated Liam McQueen.

Look for Hayden and Liam's story in The Quarterback Sneak. Coming soon.

About the Author

Liz Matis is a mild manner accountant by day and romance author by night. Married 28 years, she believes in happily-ever-after!

Fun Fact: Liz read her first romance at the age of fifteen and soon after wrote her first romances starring her friends and their latest crushes!

Fun Fact 2: Liz kept an inspiration board for Huddle Up on Pinterest. Check it out here:
http://www.pinterest.com/lizmatis/

Keep in touch with Liz

Blog:

http://www.taoofliz.blogspot.com

Email:

elizabethmatis@gmail.com

Twitter:

@LizMatis

Facebook:

Liz Matis Fan Page

https://www.facebook.com/pages/Liz-Matis-Fan-Page/308197599253896?fref=ts

Goodreads:

http://www.goodreads.com/author/show/5289185.Liz_Matis

Read Samantha And Ryan's story...

Playing For Keeps ("Fantasy" Football – Season 1) by Liz Matis

Winner of the NECRWA First Kiss Contest

Journalist Samantha Jameson always wanted to be one of the boys, but Ryan Terell won't let her join the club.

Ryan Terell is a playmaker on and off the field, but when Samantha uncovers his moves, he throws out the playbook. Just as he claims his sweetest victory, Samantha's investigation into a steroid scandal involving his team forces him to call a time-out to their off the record trysts. But then a life threatening injury on the field will force them both to decide just how far they'll go to win the game.

Read Hannah and Jake's story...

Going For It ("Fantasy" Football – Season 2) by Liz Matis

Pro football player Jake Miller's game plan for winning back supermodel Hannah Hahn is play action in the bedroom. Once he sees beyond the swimsuits and lingerie, feelings of love blindside him, changing the rules of the game.

Hannah owns the runway, but that success came with a price and a secret that's kept her from trusting a man until Jake crashes through her defenses.

The paparazzi love the beauty and the beast couple but the tabloid rumors turn ugly and test the fragile trust between them. Then Hannah loses an ad campaign to fashion's new 'it' girl. Her desperate reaction will cause Jake to challenge everything she's ever believed about herself.

Also:

Love By Design by Liz Matis

Design Intervention starts the second season with its own surprise makeover. Interior designer Victoria Bryce must break in her temporary co-host, Aussie Russ Rowland.

Sparks fly on camera as they argue over paint colors and measurement mishaps leading to passions igniting behind the scenes. But when their pasts collide with the present will the foundation they built withstand the final reveal? An HGTV meets Sex and the City romp!

Real Men Don't Drink Appletinis by Liz Matis

Hollywood's handsomest men surround celebrity agent Ava Gardner but none are as intriguing as larger-than-life Grady O'Flynn. The Navy SEAL is on an unsanctioned mission when they end up starring in their own romantic comedy.

Will they continue to sizzle when Grady has to report back to duty? In this sexy novelette by Liz Matis, two lovers have two weeks to find out.

Coming Soon:

The Quarterback Sneak ("Fantasy" Football – Season 4)

www.ingramcontent.com/pod-product-compliance
Lightning Source LLC
Chambersburg PA
CBHW060437130626
46555CB00005B/2403